THE WINK OF THE MONA LISA

ohammad Al Murr is a native of the United Arab Emirates and studied at Syracuse University in the United States. He has contributed to many Arabic newspapers and magazines and worked in financial and journalistic management. He has published twelve collections of short stories and one book on the local dialect of the UAE.

A previous collection of Mohammad Al Murr's short stories, translated into English by Dr Peter Clark OBE, was published under the title *Dubai Tales*.

ack Briggs has spent most of his working life in the Middle East, where he has acquired an extensive knowledge and understanding of the Arab language and culture. He was born in London in 1920 but grew up in Lancashire. He served with the Palestine Police from 1941 to 1948, and has been in the Gulf since 1949, becoming Commandant of Police for Dubai in 1965. While holding this important post, Jack obtained his BA in Classical and Modern Arabic as an external student of London University.

Now retired, he and his wife live in Dubai.

D1213983

THE WINK OF THE MONA LISA

and other stories from the Gulf

MOHAMMAD AL MURR

translated by Jack Briggs

MOTIVATE
PUBLISHING

Published by Motivate Publishing

Dubai: PO Box 2331, Dubai, UAE
Tel: (04) 824060, Fax: (04) 824436
E-mail: motivate@emirates.net.ae

Abu Dhabi: PO Box 43072, Abu Dhabi, UAE
Tel: (02) 271666, Fax: (02) 271888

London: Macmillan House, 96 Kensington High Street, London W8 4SG
Tel: (0171) 937 7733/937 4024, Fax: (0171) 937 7293

Published 1994
First softback edition 1998

© 1994 Mohammad Al Murr, Jack Briggs and Motivate Publishing

ISBN I 86063 076 6

British Library Cataloguing-in-Publication Data.
A catalogue record for this book is available
from the British Library.

Printed by Rashid Printing Press, Ajman, UAE

CONTENTS

PREFACE

This is the second published collection of the short stories of Mohammad Al Murr, translated from Arabic. They originally appeared in newspapers and magazines widely circulated throughout the Gulf region, and in collected form in Arabic, and have been critically acclaimed in the Arab literary world, including the BBC Arabic service.

I have known the author since he was a young man, but I did not read his creative work until a local Arab friend gave me two of his early collections. The fascination thus kindled ended in a close friendship, culminating in this publication.

For me, these stories evoke deeply-rooted aspects of my own life, the adult part of which has been spent in the Arab World. Firstly, there is my interest in the Arabic language (which now seems to dominate most other aspects); secondly, my admiration for the people of the Gulf as they were when I first came here so many years ago.

Up to the middle of this century, the effort of survival in the Gulf had created characters with tremendous resistance to adversity, in all its facets, and with great pride in their origins and traditions. The extent of their hospitality, their impeccable manners and their code of conduct, given the unrelenting austerity of their lives at that time, were incredible. Nevertheless, they were human, with very human feelings and failings. One of the great strengths of Mohammad Al Murr's tales is that they allow the reader to see all sides of the characters of those people, and the characters of their descendants in a totally modern environment.

Translating these stories has been a pleasure for me. I want to express my gratitude to Mohammad, in the first place for allowing me to translate a selection of his work, and secondly for all his assistance and co-operation; and to Chuck Grieve of Motivate Publishing for editing, prior to publication. I also have Mohammad and his stories to thank for helping me acquire yet another interest — that of reading short stories in English.

Jack Briggs

THE NIGHT'S CATCH

he target for the three boys was quite clearly defined and the anticipated spoils were tantalising. What was important to the matter in hand was that there should be careful preparation. Aboud Fateelah carried out a topographical survey of the theatre of operation.

"The house has three rooms. The third of these is the kitchen, on top of which is the pigeon-house. Between the kitchen and the other two rooms is a large almond tree. The wall of the house is old and is constructed of mud lightly coated with cement. The wall has two wooden doors; a door in the east which is the largest and a door to the west which is the smallest; both of them have two bolts so that each can be locked or opened from the outside and the inside. A fish-trap and a large, steel barrel are standing by the side of the small door."

Khalood Tanak concentrated on the booty. He made friends with the young brother of the owner of the house, expressing his admiration for the pairs of pigeons which his brother was rearing. On several occasions he bought barley and went with the young brother to feed the pigeons in order to examine the site. He then produced the following report:

"In the pigeon house are thirty pairs, most of them of a common strain except for ten pedigree pairs, mixed between 'Muffed', 'Roller', 'Carrier' and 'Fantail'. The pigeon-house has a cover made from palm fronds and small, metal walls. However, the cages are a mixture of wooden tea-boxes and metal barrels, discarded by the water sellers because of some defect or hole. The whole thing is covered with fine wire-mesh netting."

Khamaas Cola had studied the behaviour and conduct of the owner of the pigeons. He warned the others that caution would be needed:

"Humaid, the son of Shamooh, is a vindictive fisherman. I once saw him, with my own eyes, thrash three Pakistanis in a cafe near the date market. They say that he has fought a medium-sized shark with a knife and that when he is angry he shows no mercy to anyone. He thrashes everyone including his brother and his sisters, and on one occasion he actually hit his own mother in the eye with his clenched fist, because she was late in bringing him his breakfast."

The two colleagues of Khamaas shuddered when they heard these stories and his description of Humaid's character. If he had struck his mother, whom he loved, and from whom his surname was taken, because she had been late in serving his breakfast, then what would he do to those who stole his pigeons, about which he boasted in front of his friends and neighbours? Aboud Fateelah proposed cancelling the operation because of the extent of the danger involved and said:

"Let us look for someone else's pigeons. Humaid, the son of Shamooh, is a devil and a criminal and if he caught one of us he would either kill him, put his eye out or break his arm. Why should we risk our lives?"

Khalood Tanak, who had seen the booty and was unable to resist the temptation, objected:

"We have already taken pigeons from houses which were more impregnable than the house of Humaid, the son of Shamooh, houses where there were more people, some with terrifying dogs. The house of this fisherman, if he is not there himself, is one of the easiest of houses, and he has numerous pairs of pedigree pigeons which are very valuable."

Khamaas Cola, siding with Khalood Tanak, said:

"Khalood's right; what is important is to observe the house and to ensure that the criminal, Humaid, is not there when we take the pigeons."

They kept the house of Humaid, the son of Shamooh, under observation for three weeks. They learned that the mother and her children would get ready for bed between half past ten and eleven o'clock. If Humaid did not put to sea, he would sit up in the cafe, next to the gold market, until half past eleven. However, if he did go to sea he would remain on board his boat fishing, with one of his relatives, until shortly before the sun rose when they would come back with their catch to the fish market. He would return to the house only after sunrise. The three friends realised that their golden opportunity would be when Humaid went to sea and left things clear for them to carry out their operation in safety, with ease and confidence.

— 2 —

One misty autumn morning, Khamaas Cola learnt from a relative of Humaid that the pair of them would put to sea the following night. He rushed off to his two colleagues, and they held a quick but important meeting on the benches of the Al Amaana grocery near the house of Aboud Fateelah in order to discuss the raid on the house of Humaid, the son of Shamooh. The aim would be to seize as many pairs of pigeons as possible, particularly the rare and valuable pairs. They agreed that the assault must be carried out in a disciplined fashion, following a precise plan, which would ensure that the mother and the children sleeping in the large room would not awaken and also that no attention would be attracted from any passers-by. The house must be kept under observation from ten o'clock onwards in order to confirm that all the lights had been put out and that everyone had gone to sleep. After that, both doors should be bolted from the outside so that the people in the house would be unable to pursue them if they became aware of their presence. This would give them more confidence; the young brother, his sisters and his mother were unlikely to wake up, but, even of they did, they would then be able to do no more than shout and scream, and would be unable to chase the three companions. Climbing over the enclosure to the house would be done from the east wall because it was not high. Khamaas Cola would remain as a guard outside the house, to confirm that the sidestreets were clear of passers-by and to protect and warn his two colleagues in the event of the appearance of any stranger. He would wear a red-coloured *ghutra* on his head and walk along firmly and sedately, carrying a thick long stick to appear like an old man. The warning signal would be the bark of a dog, to tell the two colleagues to keep silent and alert.

— 3 —

On the night of the assault it was pitch black. At eleven o'clock, the group, when they had confirmed that all the lights of the house had been extinguished and that the mother, her daughters and young son were without doubt sleeping soundly, crept towards the house. Khamaas Cola, with his red *ghutra*, his strange gait and his long stick, began to patrol around the house. Aboud Fateelah and Khalood Tanak climbed up the east wall of the house from where they leaped on to the kitchen roof. Aboud switched on a small hand torch and shone it towards the pigeon house. The pigeons became disturbed and agitated and began to bang their heads against the cages. Khalood opened the first cage and started to seize the pigeons quickly and proficiently. He pinioned the wings to prevent the pigeon from moving. Both of the two companions had tied the ends of their long *thoubs* up to their waists, converting the *thoubs* into two large bags into which they began to toss the pinioned pigeons. Khalood put four pairs into his bag and Aboud six pairs. In the middle of the operation they heard the sound of a dog bark and threw themselves down on the kitchen roof. One of Humaid's neighbours was going down the sidestreet, coming from a nearby house. The movement of the pigeons had aroused his attention and he turned his head towards the pigeon house. After the two companions had thrown themselves down onto the roof the pigeons calmed down, but the neighbour continued to direct his gaze towards the pigeon house. Aboud then let out the sound of a female cat mewing, calling for a tomcat. The neighbour smiled and went on his way. The two companions breathed a sigh of relief. At that moment they heard a sharp, continuous barking from their friend. They were surprised; what was he barking for? The neighbour had gone. No doubt he was hurrying them on. What was the hurry for when the operation had been completed in record time and everything was just as it should be? The scoundrel; no doubt he was rushing them because he wanted to get his hands on his share.

The two companions did not realise that Khamaas was warning

them both of impending disaster. Humaid had changed his mind at the last moment because he had heard from one of his friends that the Deira cinema was showing the Indian film *Ram Aur Shyam* that night and, as he very much admired Indian films, had decided to put off going to sea until the following night. Instead, he went to see the film, which he enjoyed enormously. When he returned to his house he was surprised to find that the east door was locked by the outside bolt. He didn't think too much about this; it was probably the action of one of those wilful boys. He opened the outside metal bolt, then caught hold of the rope attached to the inside wooden bolt and pulled it. He entered the house and bolted the door from the inside. He became aware of some movement at the pigeon house. Just before the two companions withdrew Aboud switched on the hand torch for a moment, to check the point of descent. Humaid saw the light and screamed in an angry, strident voice:

"Thieves, robbers, they are stealing the pigeons!"

When the two friends heard his shouts they leaped in alarm from the roof of the kitchen to the east wall, just like Tarzan and his apes when they were climbing trees. Humaid went back to the east door and quickly opened the inside wooden bolt, but the door would not open. The sentry, Khamaas, had courageously played his part fully and had again closed the metal bolt outside. Humaid left it and went to the other door. It was also locked from the outside. He went back to the east door to climb over it. When the two friends had jumped from the wall, alarmed and confused, two pigeons had fallen out of Aboud's *thoub* and has been left lying on their backs. The two friends fled in different directions. As for Khamaas, he walked, with his red *ghutra* covering most of his face, and with his long stick, through the alleys leading to the sea. After a short while Humaid passed him, running. He asked him if some thieving boys had gone that way, and Khamaas indicated a direction different to the one which his two companions had taken.

— 4 —

The three friends met in a wooden room by the side of the house of Aboud Fateelah. His mother sometimes rented it to Indians, but it was empty that month. When they arrived they were panting from their efforts. Khamaas said, triumphantly:

"I managed to save you."

In amazement, Khalood said:

"The dog, how did he manage to come back from the sea by that time, he must be a wizard."

Aboud said, in explanation:

"He's neither a wizard nor anything else. It is certain that he never went to sea. Perhaps a storm came up or perhaps the engine of his boat broke down before he put to sea and he went to the cafe as usual."

They switched on the electric light and took off their white *thoubs* and took the booty out of them. The *thoubs* were full of pigeon droppings. They checked the pigeons. The result was four pairs of common pigeons, one Roller cock, three Muffed hens, two Carrier cocks and four Fantail hens. During the check they realised that two had fallen out while they were jumping and running after being surprised by Humaid. After assessing the booty, the three friends had a long, involved discussion on the division of the spoils, interspersed with mutual accusations of fraud, greed and theft. However, it was finally agreed, at the end of all the discussion, that all the pairs of common pigeons should be sold. Khalood should keep a single, Muffed hen, because he already had a cock of the same pedigree, Aboud should keep a Roller cock. Khamaas should keep a single Fantail hen because he wanted to buy a cock to match her from the profits of the sale of the pigeons. The remaining balance of the different kinds of pigeons should be sold.

They decided to get rid of the loot that night, as was their usual custom, because any delay would lead to many problems, including the possibility of being detected and also further disagreement about the division of the spoils. The ready purchaser, who would not ask too many questions, was available; the sole negative point was the low price which would be offered. They had no choice. At one o'clock they were knocking on the door of the house of Saloumah. After a short time she opened the door, cautiously, and peeped out, her green scarf covering her white hair and her wrinkled, black face-mask concealing the whole of her face except for her flashing eyes. She was pleased when she saw the two closed cartons. She welcomed the companions into the kitchen adjacent to her bedroom and poured out coffee for them as she began to examine the spoils. Then she said:

"We are all of a kind, and we know each other. The common pigeons, two and a half dirhams each, the Fantail pigeons, five dirhams each and the remaining pigeons, irrespective of pedigree, three dirhams apiece."

Aboud tried to protest and argue but Saloumah said, angrily:

"Not a single fil more. If you don't like the price, off you go and goodbye!"

She began to put the pigeons back in the cartons, but Khalood grabbed her hand and said:

"Don't put the pigeons back; we agree."

Saloumah said, with the smile of someone who knew she was going to win anyway:

"Good. I'll go to the room and bring the money."

Each companion got fifteen dirhams. They went to a nearby mosque and washed the pigeon droppings off their clothes and then went back to their houses with the pigeons which they were to keep and the cash.

— 5—

When Humaid was passing the fish market the next day he spotted his pigeons with Saloumah. Seething with anger, he traded insults with her and accused her of buying stolen pigeons. But she paid him back twofold; in front of everyone she insulted him and cursed his mother, his sisters and his whole family. He would have hit her if it hadn't been for the presence of dozens of men and women who were watching the show.

Humaid went away and returned a short time afterwards, accompanied by a tall policeman. Saloumah began to talk to the policeman:

"This fisherman is a maniac. He wants to know from where I bought this pigeon or that one. I live by buying and selling. Daily I buy from thousands of people; Indians; Arabs; Persians; old people; young people; men; women; how can I remember their faces when I don't know most of them?"

Then she softened her voice and said tearfully:

"This man has no shame, he cannot find anyone to fight with except me, a poor old woman as old as his grandmother. Why doesn't he go and fight with men who are more able and stronger? He wishes to oppress me, a weak old woman."

The passers-by and the policeman all sympathised with Saloumah and Humaid, after all the protests, screaming and threatening, was compelled to buy from her, at a heavy price, some of his pigeons which he loved dearly, especially those with little chicks which were still in the cages. He paid her the money while he choked with exasperation and anger.

The three friends enjoyed themselves with the money they had gained from the night's catch. They spent the morning in a games parlour, playing the pin-ball and slot machines and they had a lunch of *biriyani* and *dhal* in an Indian restaurant. In the evening, happy and carefree, they clapped and shouted as they followed the fierce battles in *Ram Aur Shyam* at the Deira cinema.

THE IMPORTANT DECISION

When Aisha awoke, the hands of the clock were pointing to six. Daylight filled most of her small room and she sat up on her bed. She felt very disheartened and the chirping of the birds annoyed her. Why were they so active at daybreak? Then she remembered the important decision which she had been thinking about all the previous evening. What was life all about? Just a series of decisions... For her part, Aisha always tried to take wise and intelligent decisions, but she believed that the decisions taken by other people in matters which involved her, sometimes through bad luck or just ill-fate and sometimes out of sheer hatred or plain dislike, were not generally in her interests. Suddenly she felt cold — she was always going to turn down the air-conditioning and then she would forget — and she jumped off the bed and went towards the air-conditioning unit, but then turned aside towards the bathroom and switched the light on. She looked at her face in the bathroom mirror. Her nose was a little big, but she was good-looking. Yesterday one of her old school friends had got married and when Aisha had been at the wedding she had been struck by how ugly the bride was. She remembered, even when they had been in the intermediate school, that the other girl had hardly been what you would call a beauty queen, but she would have expected that feminine maturity would have produced a few more attractive features for her. The bridegroom was her paternal cousin and it appeared to be an arrangement made by the family.

Aisha was highly critical of her own family. She only had one cousin and he had married a long time ago. Why had her own uncles not produced more boys, older than she was, or at least of the same age, so that one of them could have married her? She lifted her hair up over her head. Her neck was long. She turned to the right and looked at her profile in the three-way bathroom mirror. The sight displeased her because of her big nose; she never looked good in a side-view photograph. She smiled; her teeth were white and even, but what good was that? Up to now nobody had come forward asking to marry the possessor of those fine, white, even teeth. She remembered a story she had read about the faithfulness of Arab women. It was about a woman, renowned for the beauty of her mouth and teeth, who, after the death of her husband, had received a proposal of marriage. She broke off her teeth and sent them to her suitor as a symbol of her fidelity to the memory of her deceased husband. Aisha couldn't remember the moral of the story. If she had been the woman she would have accepted the new husband, for life was short; why should we hang on to the past? How could the dead husband benefit from that painful act, always supposing that the story was true? Very often she was sceptical about the stories of heroism and virtue which she read. The atmosphere in which she lived was as far away as it could be from such matters.

She looked at her slightly protruding ears. One of her friends had had cosmetic surgery on her ears to have them set closer to her head. In fact, Aisha didn't need such an operation, first because she was afraid of operations anyway and also because her hair was thick and covered the protrusion of her ears. Her eyes were large and black, and were the first thing that most of the young men whom she had known had complimented her on. However, that opinion was not universal. At secondary school she had been afraid of one of the fat dark-skinned girls in her class who was often sarcastic about the size of her eyes and used to say that they were like "the eyes of a cow which has seen something on fire."

Ever since she had been quite small, Aisha had always sought praise and commendation. When her mother wanted her to undertake a task which might be difficult for her, she would never have to threaten or slap her. It was enough for her to say, "Get up, my sweetie, and do so and so," or "Get up, my pretty one, and make such and such." Even her classmates in school knew of this soft spot of hers and took full advantage of it. One of them might say, in front of all the others, "If beauty could be measured by percentage I would give Aisha ninety per cent." By doing so she would ensure that she would be able to give Aisha the three pieces of material which she had just bought and that Aisha would pay for them to be made up for her. This was why she was hurt by the fat girl's sarcastic criticism of her eyes.

She sat down on the wooden bathroom stool and looked at her feet. On the heel of the right foot was some thickened tissue; she washed it, reached out for the thick black sponge and rubbed at her heel until she had removed the tissue. She saw a big black ant moving towards her left foot. The damned thing wanted to bite her! She gave it a bang with the edge of her sandal and split it into two pieces. Each piece curled over for a moment and then stopped moving. The bite of one of those accursed ants could be really painful. No matter how much eau de cologne and powder she applied, it would always make her leg swell and she would then be rubbing it for days. After she left the bathroom she sat down in front of the big mirror in the reception room. She didn't know why, but that mirror made her appear prettier than the one in the bathroom.

She would tell Salim about her important decision: their relationship must come to an end. Last night she had looked back thoroughly at it. A loving relationship that had lasted for two years was no easy matter to bring to an end. Their first encounter had been quite commonplace. He had come to cash a cheque in the branch of the bank where she worked, and she had been sitting at the information desk. However, the passage of time and the development of their relationship had added, for them, mythical and romantic connotations to the encounter. Their meetings were erratic, as he was living in Abu Dhabi while she was living in Dubai; however, the gaps only served to fuel the passion and longing. Salim was a good listener to her long chats full of gossip. Once, when he had drawn some compensation money from the government, he had bought her a diamond necklace, the same as the one he had bought for his wife. On another occasion, when she was admitted to hospital for a few days with food poisoning, he tricked the hospital authorities, claiming to be her brother, and managed to visit her several times.

In spite of all these things, all the niceties, the delights, the flirting and the gifts which crowned their relationship, he gave her to understand, in no uncertain terms, that there were three important points on which he would never change his mind. Firstly, he loved his children, secondly, he respected his wife, and thirdly, the possibility of his taking a second wife was out of the question. Although Aisha had believed that it was possible for Salim to change his mind about these three things, especially the last, it was now patently clear to her that this belief was both delusive and fanciful. She had even indicated that she would not be offended by becoming the second wife, but Salim paid no attention. She thought, once, in a moment of desperation, of allowing herself to become pregnant by him and presenting him with a *fait accompli*, so that he would have to marry her. However, she dropped this idea; a marriage which took place under the threat of disgrace would be miserable.

What a wretched and despicable situation she was in; why did she have to be so unlucky and unhappy? Of the two young men with whom she had had relationships before she met Salim, the first was handsome, narcissistic and arrogant, seeing himself as a star of beauty which should circle the world in its own orbit, and his view of her, putting it mildly, had been the view of a master toward his maidservant; he had never once touched upon the subject of marriage. However, the second was unbearably stupid and dull-witted; his conversation was boring, while his jokes were sickening. Lie to him and he would believe you; deceive him and he could be led along like a lamb to the slaughter. If only he had possessed just some outward signs of charm she could have considered leading him on to marriage, but, as well as being stupid, he was quite ugly. She was always followed by bad luck. She never understood why; she had never harmed anyone in her life. She always took part in all the social and charitable activities, she loved children, and she never passed any beggars, male or female, without giving them something, whether they actually asked for it or not.

After she had finished dressing and had put on her make-up, she went into the dining room. She saw the Sri Lankan servant girl adjusting her mother's face-mask. She kissed her mother on the head and hands and sat down to eat her breakfast of a half slice of bread, a little butter and jam and hot tea with milk. She never liked a big breakfast; when she got hungry at the office; at ten or eleven o'clock, she would distract herself with a few nuts and lots of cups of tea. She looked at her mother; her mask was shiny, as were her eyes. The stroke three years ago had left her permanently paralysed. She had spoken, with difficulty, for a time, but then she had stopped talking altogether. The doctor told them that if she had really wanted to walk and talk, and had made an effort to do so, then she would have been able to, but it appeared as though she had lost the spirit to fight her illness and she subsequently never moved or spoke; she just withdrew from the active world.

In the early days of her mother's affliction, Aisha, too, succumbed to her feelings and would cry every day for hours, but she no longer worried too much about her mother and left her alone with her chair, the maidservant and the television, which she watched incessantly. Her mother had been married three times and her paternal aunt had married twice. Her father had also married twice, while her maternal uncle had been married three times. When Aisha spoke to her friend Badriya, who worked for one of the ladies' societies, about this phenomenon, Badriya explained it as simply a matter of supply and demand, just as in economics. Before oil was found, the men had been compelled to accept whoever was available locally and to marry from within their own community because travel abroad was not possible for the vast majority. As a result, spinsterhood did not present a problem and there were few women who remained divorcees. As for the number of times that people got married in those days, most marriages were arranged without the parties having known each other previously and if, after the wedding, the two were satisfied with each other and accepted the situation, then the marriage continued. If, however, they didn't find each other compatible, then they divorced, with both parties knowing full well that a marriage for a second or a third time was not going to be either a difficult or an impossible matter, particularly if they were both young, because of the total lack of any outside supply. She had heard from one of the religious men that, in the early days of Islam, a woman used to propose marriage to a man. She thought this over. But if she went and offered herself in marriage to one of the neighbours' sons whom she thought might be nice, without there having been any previous relationship, her story would be a huge joke and she would be the laughing stock of the whole of Dubai.

After breakfast she went back to her room to get her handbag. Her grey cat was stretched out under the bed, totally relaxed, mewing away, while her five kittens sucked noisily at her rosy teats with their eyes still closed. Aisha smiled; her cat had given birth only four days before, her third litter… she thought of her sister who had become pregnant and had turned the matter of her pregnancy into a major drama, forcing the whole family to share her concern. What would she have done if she had been like the cat and had given birth, every time, to five or six kittens? Before she left the house she gave instructions to the servant girl to feed the cat.

— 2 —

Her car had not been in the garage for servicing for four months, and when she started it up in the mornings it would give out a disagreeable sound and shudder violently for a few moments. As she went past the graveyard near the Creek, she read a notice on the wall advertising one of the trading companies: "The last chance to benefit from the big sale at the Fun and Leisure Store" and immediately felt depressed. She thought of Salim. What was his response going to be when she told him her important decision? Would he oppose it, be offended or ask her not to be hasty? Would he ask her if she was in love with someone else, and would he cry and seek reconciliation? Or would he agree with her decision ? She just did not know.

She had to stop for the red light at one of the sets of traffic lights. Her life was confused and in turmoil; just what she was going to do after this she did not know. She began to feel very distressed and suddenly tears were running down her face. The lights changed from red to green but she didn't notice; she was wiping her tears from her eyes and face. One after the other the cars behind her hooted, prompting her to move on. Damn you, what are you all in such a hurry for? You are only going from one misery to another. She got her car moving and looked at herself in the mirror. Her tears had destroyed her eye-shadow and make-up, which upset her.

When she got to the bank she went straight to the bathroom and repaired her face. In the loans section, where she was now working, a young man, a heavy drinker, sat opposite her. Even in the mornings his breath smelled of whisky. He couldn't talk about anything except football. His jokes were about football; anything serious which he had to say was about football. Nothing in the world mattered to him except football. If ever a miracle happened and football was banned, then he would commit suicide out of grief and despair. On her right hand side sat a skinny girl who had recently got married. All she could ever talk about was her husband, Abu Shihab. It was Abu Shihab said this and Abu Shihab did that — Abu Shihab loves chicken — Abu Shihab went to Kuwait for three days — Abu Shihab is bound to be promoted this year. Aisha felt that the girl deliberately went on and on about her husband just to irritate her. A number of times she was on the point of telling her that she and her Abu Shihab could go to hell but then she controlled herself by saying to herself that the husband would soon tire of the girl, while she would get fed up with the husband too after a while.

Things were no different that morning. As usual, she had to listen to her workmate telling her, in great pain and distress, about the team which he was supporting being knocked out of the championship series because everyone else was plotting against the team to prevent them from winning the championship: all the other clubs, the referees and the linesmen, the football association and even the people who made up the occult amulets and magic charms. Meanwhile, the girl next to her showed her, at least four times, the gold bangles which Abu Shihab had bought for her the day before, pointing out how marvellous the workmanship was and how brilliant the design and form of the bangles.

She was rescued by the telephone from having to hear the girl's hymns of praise to Abu Shihab's good taste. It was her friend Faiza, who told her about the sale at the Fun and Leisure Store. Faiza's salary was more than Aisha's; in spite of this, she was mean and checked the price of everything and never bought anything except at the sales. Faiza had talked to her once about this philosophy. The likelihood of her ever getting married was poor; she had already passed the age of twenty-nine and she was of a temperamental nature. Through her own stupidity she had already missed three golden chances of marriage. When her father died (and this was not likely to be for some time yet because the members of his family always lived to a ripe old age) she wouldn't inherit anything worth mentioning because she had many brothers, and anyway she doubted if he would be leaving very much because he was a spendthrift who had never been very careful in the handling of his money. Therefore, she had only her job, in which she tried to climb her way up by means of cunning and opportunism, although she often faltered during her climb due to her stupidity. She relied on what she could manage to save during her working life. Aisha had often thought of breaking off her friendship with Faiza, because of her temperament, opportunism and meanness, but then she would change her mind and decide just not to talk to her for three or four days. She was aware of a sort of obscure, mutual affection between them; they shared a similar situation. Faiza accepted it in her own fashion, whilst Aisha attempted to change it and fight against it in her own special way. Faiza's concerns were materialistic and practical, whilst Aisha read poetry and novels, wrote her journal and joined in social activities. Faiza made an enemy of the world and showed no gratitude for any compassion; Aisha still loved the world and wanted its affection and friendship.

When Aisha returned to the house, some time after two o'clock, she ate nothing but a little fruit, which was unusual for her. She went to her bedroom and threw herself down, thinking about her important decision.

— 3 —

When Salim opened the door of his American car, Aisha caught the scent of perfume. She got in and greeted him, smiling. Salim took her two hands in his and kissed both palms and her heart bounded. They moved off. She talked to him about her grey cat giving birth to five kittens whose eyes were still unopened, she told him about the antics of her pregnant sister and she read him her journal of the previous week. Then she informed him of the latest report from the doctor on her mother's condition. The anecdotes poured out like little streams, filling the river of Aisha's heart with delight and joy.

— 4 —

It was nine o'clock in the evening when Salim stopped his car by the side of her car. He took her two hands and kissed the palm of her right hand, then the palm of her left hand, and said:

"Next Thursday?"

"Yes."

"Six o'clock?"

"Yes."

She blew him a kiss and got out. She slipped into her car and turned the ignition key; her car shook, shuddering as if it were dancing. She remembered that she hadn't told Salim about her important decision. She smiled; never mind, she'd tell him next time.

THE AWESOME LADY

hen she was small her father used to take her into his *majlis*, which was always crowded with traders, pearl merchants, masters of dhows and men of religion, and he was always referred to as 'the father of Shamsa'. If one of the pearl merchants was trying to get her father to increase his offer on the pearls he was buying from him he would swear on 'the head of Shamsa'. When the incense burner was brought to the *majlis* it was always given to Shamsa before anyone else. Their large house at Ras Deira had at least twenty slaves. The number of persons who would eat in her father's *majlis*, on the various social occasions, would exceed one hundred.

However, the good times did not last. One after the other, disasters struck, dire misfortunes which threatened to bring to an end the family of Shamsa. Her father lost the whole of his fortune when the pearl market collapsed. When he died they did not find a single rupee in his big chest and they had to sell one of the big mirrors from his house to buy his burial shroud. Shamsa married twice. The first marriage lasted two months, after which she arranged a divorce because her husband would speak to her harshly and she could not bear it. He was the son of one of the smaller pearl merchants whose existence had depended on the wealth of her father and his commercial dealings. The second time was for one month, after which she was divorced because her second husband was just a mean employee who refused to buy her scents and perfumes. The good-for-nothing, what was his standing compared with hers!

She received no inheritance from her father except the Big House. The slaves, the entourage, the people, the guests and the clamour, had all disappeared. Only she herself and her two slaves, Saloum and Rumaanah, remained at the house. She constructed doors from the big *majlis* on to the street and divided it into five shops which she rented to five Indian traders. She then cut herself off from people and the world.

— 2 —

The years passed, and Shamsa had no contact with the outside world except through her slave Saloum and one of the Indian perfume dealers, Suliman, who used to bring the rent for the five shops to her each year and sometimes brought scent and incense when she asked for it.

Once, when one of the traders from Ras Deira died, there were whispers that his wife had poisoned him with poison which she had got from this dealer. However, these whispers died away after the wife had donated one half of the inheritance from her husband to the poor and some charitable causes.

— 3 —

Saloum told her about the steamers which were now coming into the Creek, but she was uninterested. He also told her about the electricity which was now lighting the houses. She wouldn't have it in the Big House which she continued to light with kerosene lamps in just two rooms only, out of the ten rooms in the house: the small servants' room on the ground floor and her own room on the top floor. The house was dark, even during the day. After Shamsa isolated herself she nailed up all the windows in the house, on both the top and bottom floors. She had an old radio which she switched on only occasionally. When Saloum talked breathlessly to her about a new radio, in which you could see people while they were talking, walking, wrestling, singing and dancing, she didn't show the slightest bit of curiosity, either to know more about it or to possess it. As for all the other new things which they told her about, the bridge, the motor-cars, the aeroplanes, the schools, the new clothes, the new markets and so on, she showed no enthusiasm for them at all.

— 4 —

The 'awesome lady' liked neither Saloum nor Rumaanah. All the intelligent slaves had abandoned the Big House. Tufouh, of whom she had been extremely fond and with whom she had played when she was a child, and whose clothes had been made from the same material as her own clothes, had left her and had fled to Kuwait where she had married. The slave Khamaas, who used to make her laugh a great deal with his jokes and stories, so much so that she could not bear to be separated from him, had abandoned the house and gone to sea on one of the dhows. The good-looking slave Jasoum had also left her. His facial features, his lips and nose, were handsome, with no distinctive negroid attributes, apart from the fact that he was black. In fact, Tufouh had once whispered to her that he might even be her brother. At any rate, they used to buy clothes for him of the same kind as they bought for her only brother, Obaid, who had been drowned in the Creek after drinking several glasses of Iranian *araq*. They had all gone. All the slaves she had been fond of had left her. They had left the Big House. They were scattered between the decks of ships, oil wells and the houses of their new masters.

Left with her were Saloum and Rumaanah, the two slaves whom she really hated. It seemed as if they didn't know where to go. They had been married when they were young and had no children. Saloum's face was always rigid and his features never relaxed except when he looked at Rumaanah, while her face was continually gloomy and never showed compassion or serenity except when she saw Saloum coming from afar. Shamsa never struck them, but what she said to them and the way she looked at them was worse than any beating, more repulsive than any torture and more humiliating than all the insults of the world. Saloum used to consider leaving the Big House often, but Rumaanah could not come to terms with this. She had spent all her life in that one house and had never left it, even for a day. All the sons and daughters of the female slaves used to spend most of their time outside the house, except Rumaanah. She was allocated for service with Shamsa's mother when she was just a child, and then with Shamsa herself. Throughout her life she had been like a small satellite, revolving in the orbit of the celestial body of the 'awesome lady' and the family of the Big House.

— 5 —

The monotony of life in the Big House did not change until Saloum told the 'awesome lady' that the owner of one of the big dhows had brought some little monkeys from Pakistan; they could play tricks, clap their hands and smoke cigarettes, and they were for sale. For the first time the curiosity of the 'awesome lady' was aroused. She asked him the price. On the following day Saloum was to be seen going in through the small opening in the massive door of the Big House, dragging behind him, on steel chains, two little monkeys. It was the first time for many years that any strange man or animal had entered the Big House. Shamsa, contrary to many of the widows and divorcees living alone, who kept cows, goats, hens and ducks, detested such animals and had a strong aversion to keeping them.

— 6 —

The 'awesome lady' was delighted with the two monkeys. There was a male and a female, and she named the male Adoul and the female Hanoun. She opened up a large room for them on the top floor near her own room. All her attention, and in consequence the attention of her two slaves, was centred on Adoul and Hanoun from then on. They used to feed the two of them pistachios and titbits as well as all kinds of fruit. Some they would eat and the remainder they would throw away. The 'awesome lady' raised no objection to this; indeed, she would laugh about it while feeding Saloum and Rumaanah with great austerity. At first the two monkeys were naked, but then the 'awesome lady' had two dresses made for Hanoun from an expensive silk material and two sets of embroidered shirts and baggy trousers for Adoul from a highly-priced cloth. Saloum and Rumaanah had never dreamt of wearing clothing comparable in either the splendid style or the high price to the clothing of the two monkeys.

The 'awesome lady' lost her sense of reason with her fondness for Hanoun and Adoul and even went so far as to buy golden jewellery for Hanoun's hands and neck. Twenty years before, she had bought one single gold ring for Rumaanah, and this was still the sole piece of jewellery which adorned her hands. After a short time the 'awesome lady' permitted Adoul and Hanoun to have their steel chains removed, whereupon they converted the house into a minor circus, full of clamour and high-pitched screaming; they would throw the furniture about and defecate in the rooms and passages. And who carried the burden of the cleaning and re-organising after all this destructive pandemonium? Saloum and Rumaanah. On top of all this, Hanoun, who was the noisiest and the most active and troublesome of the two, would jump on Rumaanah and sit on top of her head, beat her about the face and urinate on her while Rumaanah remained motionless, particularly when she was being watched by the 'awesome lady', who was amused by it all. She would laugh at Hanoun's tormenting of Rumaanah, while at a distance Saloum was seething with anger.

— 7 —

The 'awesome lady' was awakened on a cold winter's morning by a high-pitched scream coming from Adoul and Hanoun's room. She leapt up in alarm and went to the room. She saw, to her distress, Hanoun stretched out on the bed. Adoul was touching her with his finger and sniffing at her while continuing to scream shrilly. Rumaanah came running, and after a short time Saloum too arrived, showing alarm and grief. The 'awesome lady' sensed that he was smiling but her own grief distracted her from everything else.

She dressed herself all in black, buried Hanoun in the eastern corner of the compound of the Big House and declared a period of mourning just as if the death was the death of a human being. She asked Suliman the perfumer to bring the Quranic readers and they read the Quran for three nights. During those nights she spent a lot of time alone with Suliman and a lot of whispering went on between them.

— 8 —

Two weeks after the incident, at dawn, after yet another cold winter's night, the 'awesome lady' heard a sharp grief-stricken wail from Rumaanah. She adjusted her pillow below her head, smiled, then closed her eyes.

HAMDAH'S QUESTIONS

ven before we actually entered the circus tent my daughter Hamdah's questions began:

"What did you buy?"

"Two tickets for the circus."

"How much are they?"

"Seventy-five dirhams."

"But the man in front of us paid less."

"Because he bought two second-class tickets."

"What's the difference?"

"The difference is that the person who buys first-class tickets sits near the circus ring and the one who buys second-class tickets sits further away on the back seats."

"Why don't all the people buy first-class tickets so that everybody can sit near the circus ring?"

Before I could answer we had entered the circus tent and Hamdah was busy looking at the lights, the spectators and the circus workers as they organised their wires and chairs. We chose a place in the second row. In front of us, in the front row to the right, sat two German ladies with their two children. The blonde lady's little girl was only two or three years old but the dark-haired lady's daughter was eight or nine. In the front row, on the left hand side, were two young ladies wearing silk 'aba's; the first resembled an Egyptian actress, Sawsan Badr, with her brown Egyptian facial features, which were like those of the queens of the Pharaohs, while the second resembled another Egyptian actress, Suhair Ramzi, with her broad, white face, wide eyes, full lips and fine long nose. The only difference between this lady and Suhair Ramzi was that she was slimmer and more graceful than the actress and her facial features were softer and more harmonious. 'Sawsan Badr' had a little boy with her, aged about four or five years, wearing a white, full-length outer garment with a gold coloured skull-cap while 'Suhair Ramzi' had a little girl, about the same age as her companion's son, wearing a brilliant red dress, decorated with lots of white ribbons.

In our row a fat man, wearing a woollen outer garment and a brown headdress with a thick 'aqaal, sat down. He had with him more than ten children; half of them appeared to be his own, while the others were probably those of his neighbours or relatives. After they had sat down, Hamdah renewed her questioning:

"Why doesn't the circus begin?"

"They are waiting for all the empty seats to be filled by spectators."

"Why?"

"So that they'll get more money?"

"Who are 'they'?"

"The owners of the circus."

"Are they rich?"

"I don't know."

Immediately after this question the floodlights illuminated the stage in the middle of the circus tent, the music struck up and an olive-skinned man of average height with curly hair appeared. He was wearing a shiny white suit and white top hat, and had a microphone in his right hand and a gleaming white stick in his left. He addressed us in a loud voice, in English, with a foreign accent:

"I welcome you all, ladies, gentlemen and my dear children, to the great Italian circus, the circus of Nicoli, which comes to you, in Dubai, from Italy for the very first time. You will witness, in this enjoyable display, the acrobats with their exciting and thrilling feats, the magicians with their unprecedented performance which defies belief and the clowns in their amusing acts, which will leave you in prolonged fits of laughter. There will be formidable and fierce animals which the trainers will command to greet you and dance for you. For you, our appreciative audience, the circus of Nicoli has prepared all these fascinating and exhilarating performances for your pleasure and enjoyment, so, sit down in your seats and relax comfortably, as we commence with the first act, Miss Jamina, the well-known artiste from Rumania."

Hamdah grabbed me by the hand and asked:

"What is he saying?"

"He is welcoming the audience and saying that the young lady, Jamina, will present the first act."

The music struck up and Jamina entered the ring. She was short and wore a long black cloak which reached down to her knees. The audience clapped; she greeted them and went to stand in the centre of the ring. A man came and fixed onto the top of her head a small, circular disc, connected to a wire which rose up to the top of the circus tent. She was then raised several metres off the ground by the wire and took off her black cloak and threw it down to be caught by one of the workers. She now appeared in a red swimming costume and, suspended in the air, twirled her small, short body around. More applause. The wire was lowered a little and one of the men gave her a tray on which stood a teapot and a number of cups: she was raised up again. She then raised her knees, suspended as she was in the air, placed the tray on them and began to take tea from one of the cups. Applause again. Hamdah said in amazement:

"Won't she spill the tea?"

"No."

"Why not?"

"Because there is no tea in either the teapot or the cups."

"Then she is cheating us?"

"No, she is showing us that she is capable of performing that particular acrobatic movement."

The ringmaster in the white suit then appeared and said:

"Our thanks to the amazing Miss Jamina, and now, another exciting act from Miss Jelini."

A tall, blonde girl then entered, wearing a glittering white swimsuit. She was smiling as she greeted the audience. They clapped. Hamdah asked:

"Why are all the artistes undressed?"

I smiled and said:

"They wear swimsuits because they are the most suitable attire for their acrobatic movements. If they wore long dresses these would restrict them and they would become entangled in them."

Miss Jelini lay down on her back on a special bench and raised her legs. A boy, about twelve years of age, wearing a golden embroidered cloak, came along and placed a large plastic dice on the soles of her feet. She began to spin it to the sound of the music. 'Sawsan Badr' laughed at the motions of Miss Jelini playing with the dice while 'Suhair Ramzi' gave her little girl some chocolate. Next, the boy brought a long brown cylindrical drum, and Miss Jelini began to spin it and play with it on her feet, making it dance to the music. After the drum he came up with a large plastic star in all the colours of the rainbow and then a big, long pipe in blue, red and gold, which she began to spin on her feet at a tremendous speed. Said Hamdah:

"Doesn't she get tired, spinning all these things?"

"No."

"Why not?"

"Because her legs and her thighs are strong."

When Jelini had finished her act, the clowns came on and began to shake hands with the children sitting in the front row overlooking the ring.

The little girl of the blonde, German lady was afraid of the clown who came towards us but the son of 'Sawsan Badr' and the daughter of 'Suhair Ramzi' were enthusiastic about the clowns and eagerly shook hands with them, laughing as they did so. Hamdah said:

"Why do the clowns paint their faces?"

"To make us laugh."

"Can't they make us laugh without the paint?"

Some white horses then entered from a large opening on the right of the tent and the ringmaster cried out:

"The dapple-grey Appaloosa horses greet you!"

Eight dapple-grey horses circled the ring, escorted by the trainer with his whip. They halted in the centre of the ring and bowed their heads in greeting to the audience. The usual applause followed. The daughter of the German woman started crying, fearful of the horses. Her mother took her back to the second row, where they sat down beside us. The horses began to circle again but this time in pairs, and then a horse stood on its hind legs. Applause. The horses circled again in fours, stopped in the centre of the ring, bowed their heads to the audience and went out of the ring. More applause. Two new horses entered, circling the ring, and stood up on their hind legs. One of them stood up again and began to move to the music being played just as if it were dancing. Hamdah said:

"Will they ask us to ride these horses?"

"No."

"Why not?"

"Because these horses are clever and are trained in acrobatics."

"And the horses which people ride?"

"They are dumb horses."

The circus workers then brought in a metal safe and placed it in the middle of the ring. A pretty girl entered, wearing a yellow dress, took off all her heavy jewellery, which appeared to be just fake jewellery, placed it in the safe, closed it and went away. On came two clowns, dressed up as thieves. They circled around until one of them bumped into the other, and they both laughed at the accident.

They tried to open the safe but were unable to do so. Then one of them kicked the other up the rear and told him to open up the case which they had brought with them. They opened up the case and took out five firecrackers, done up to look like sticks of dynamite, which they placed before the safe and lit. The crackers went off, the safe opened and out came a dwarf clown, wearing police uniform, who arrested them. Hamdah said:

"Where has the jewellery gone?"

"With the policeman."

"Will he give it back to the lady owner?"

"I think so."

The ringmaster then cried out:

"And now, ladies, gentlemen and my dear young friends, you are about to see two beautiful young girls from South America — watch now! watch now!"

Two beautiful young girls, wearing very short black dresses, began to swallow long prongs, aflame at the end. Whenever either of them withdrew the extinguished prong from her mouth, it would flare up.

The circus workers then produced a closed box which they placed in the centre of the ring. One of the two young girls went and opened it and took out two large snakes. She wrapped one of the snakes around her neck and gave the other one to her colleague for her to do the same. The girls circled around in front of the audience with the two snakes wrapped around their necks. The son of 'Sawsan Badr' screamed while the daughter of 'Suhair Ramzi' laughed. The ringmaster then said, in a whisper:

"Ladies and gentlemen, these snakes are extremely dangerous, they are of the poisonous variety and a single bite from one means instant death to man. Now watch! Watch! The kiss of death."

Then one of the two girls lifted up the big snake which she was carrying, caught hold of its head and kissed it on the mouth as she smiled. There was applause. Hamdah asked:

"Why didn't it bite her?"

I smiled and said:

"Because it loves her."

The two girls ended their turn by blowing a burst of flame in front of them while the ringmaster cried out:

"Now we have art and beauty with the sweet and beautiful young lady, Margarita Martinez and her brother, the acrobat, Carlos Martinez."

Margarita began to climb the ladder with her brother Carlos to the platform, where each of them took hold of a long balancing pole and walked along the wire which was stretched across the top of the tent, from the right side to the very far end of the left side. Applause. On the second crossing Carlos sat down in the middle of the wire while Margarita walked with the balancing pole and passed right over the top of him, then Carlos stood on his head on the wire. The audience clapped again. Margarita placed a black cloth over her head, so that she could not see, and then walked, with the balancing pole, to the other end of the wire. There was furious clapping. Carlos sat on a chair in the middle of the wire and stood up on it while holding on to his balancing pole. Next, he stood on one leg and the ringmaster cried out:

"Ladies and gentlemen, Carlos will now attempt a very difficult feat — he will walk without the use of the balancing pole. Watch carefully!"

Carlos walked, in step with the music, up to the centre of the wire. At this point he lost his balance and fell, but managed to catch hold of the wire. The spectators screamed in sympathy and fear. Carlos then said, "thank you", speaking in Arabic and returned to a standing position on the wire. The band struck up with a dance tune, Carlos danced and clapped his hands to the music and the children began to clap with him. 'Suhair Ramzi' was clapping and laughing but 'Sawsan Badr' opened her handbag and began to renew her make-up. After the tight-wire walking it was the turn of the magicians; into the ring walked the magician, Elvis, and his blonde wife, Irma. Hamdah asked me who they were. I said:

"It is the magician Elvis and Irma, his wife, also a magician."

"Do they have any children who are magicians?"

I smiled and said:

"I don't know."

Elvis produced a small locker and put his wife inside. He passed a number of swords around the audience so that they could confirm their rigidity and then he plunged all of them into the locker. He opened the locker; all the swords which had pierced the locker could be seen, but his wife had disappeared. He closed the locker, pulled out the swords and when he opened the locker again his wife came out smiling. Applause. Hamdah said, in a confident voice:

"I knew that the wife would not be harmed by the swords!"

"How?"

"Because the husband wouldn't hurt his wife."

Elvis then produced a round silver box. Out of it he took a large red sack and some black rope. He placed his wife in the sack and tied the opening. He then put the bag and its contents into the round box, closed it and tied it with the black rope in a very precise manner. Next he took a round, red drape and covered himself with it, standing on a round box. After just a few seconds the drape was raised and his wife appeared, to applause, and when she untied the black rope, opened the box, took out the red sack, untied the knot and opened it, out came the husband. The applause increased. Hamdah said:

"How did that happen?"

"A trick of magic."

"Why are there so many flies here?"

"Flies like sweets, children and horses and in this circus all these things are gathered together."

A British performer came on, juggling with bows and wooden hoops, throwing and catching them. Then he began to play with yellow balls.

Hamdah said:

"Is he from the Al Wasl club?"

"I don't think so."

"Then why is he juggling with their yellow balls?"

"I don't think that he chose a particular colour, it's simply a coincidence."

Next the juggler took a long piece of wood between his teeth. He threw one of the balls to the audience and asked them to throw it back to him so that he could catch it with the piece of wood. Hamdah said:

"Won't his teeth break?"

"No, his teeth are strong."

He then began to juggle with three plates, throwing them up and catching them. Hamdah said:

"Do they eat off those plates?"

"No."

"Why not?"

"Because they are only for the juggling."

The workers started to hang up a large, long blue net from the left of the tent right across to the right side. Hamdah said:

"Will they catch fish with that net?"

"I don't think so."

One of the dwarf clowns passed by us and stroked Hamdah with a soft feather brush which he was carrying. She laughed with delight. Next to us was a fat youth, wearing a black gown and a blue skullcap. He was sitting as still as a statue. He didn't laugh at the antics of the clowns, nor was he interested in the acts of the magicians or the other performers. The figures and the bathing costumes of the pretty girls didn't interest him and it seemed that he was sick and tired of the whole world. I don't know why he ever came to the circus; perhaps it was because it was less disgusting than the outside world. An Indian with a tray, selling soft drinks and sweets came past and I bought some sweets for Hamdah. 'Sawsan Badr' bought a can of Pepsi for her son and 'Suhair Ramzi' bought a can of Seven-Up for her daughter. The ringmaster then called out:

"And now, ladies and gentlemen, we present to you the Flying Suza troupe, four young people from Brazil who will now fill this tent with a sensational flying trapeze act."

The four began their act using the three trapezes suspended from the top of the tent. Hamdah said:

"What would happen if they fell to the ground?"

"They would fall into the net."

"And if the net split?"

"Nothing would happen because it is close to the ground."

The enthusiasm of 'Sawsan Badr' and 'Suhair Ramzi' began to wane and they began to yawn, whereas their infants became even more enthusiastic.

One of the trapeze artistes was caught by his legs by one of the others and Hamdah said:

"What would happen if his hands were broken?"

"They would send for a doctor."

"And would they allow the doctor to come into the circus ring?"

"Yes, in such an emergency situation."

One of the female artistes flew through the air and was caught by her hands by a colleague. Hamdah said:

"What would happen if her bathing costume were to be torn off?"

"Then she would be naked."

"But that would be shameful!"

One of the artistes, having covered his face with a red cloth, leaped into the air and was caught by his colleague. Loud applause. Then they both jumped into the net to end their display.

The ringmaster announced that there would be an interval of ten minutes. Hamdah began to eat her sweets and the workers began to erect a cage made of steel rods around the ring. Hamdah said:

"Why are they making the steel cage?"

"Because they are going to bring on wild animals, like lions and tigers."

"Can't the animals break down the steel cage?"

"No, they cannot, because it is strong."

"Can't they leap over the steel cage?"

"No, they cannot."

"Why not?"

"Because the cage is high and the animals are dumb."

"But on the television they chase after all the other animals in the jungle."

"The circus is different to the jungle."

"How?"

"Because the trainer beats them."

"Why?"

"So that they will carry out the acrobatic acts."

"Can't they carry out acrobatics without being beaten."

"No."

A worker went past, spraying the ring-side with an air-freshener. Hamdah said:

"What is he spraying?"

"A perfume to freshen the air."

"Why?"

"Because the smell from the animals is abominable."

"Why?"

"Because they don't bathe."

"Why not?"

"Because they strongly dislike bathing."

The animals came on with their trainer, Yuri Nicoli, who was a handsome young man with long blond hair. There were three tigers and four lionesses. Each one sat on a stool. Hamdah said:

"It's just like school, everyone is sitting on a chair."

The trainer brought each animal, one by one, to the centre of the ring in order to make it jump over stands of various shapes and sizes. The lionesses began roaring loudly and some of the children cried. The trainer then made a pyramid out of the chairs and one of the lionesses sat on the apex. Two tigers sat on her right, and two lionesses sat lower down.

The trainer then ordered one of the tigers to walk along two ropes stretched out in the middle of the ring. At first it refused but after a few cracks of the whip the tiger walked along the two ropes in an awkward fashion. Afterwards the trainer went and kissed one of the lionesses on the mouth. Hamdah said:

"Won't she bite him?"

"No."

"Why?"

"Because he is a handsome young man with blond hair."

After the animal act the ringmaster said:

"The Nicola Circus will be in Dubai for two weeks, so visit us again or tell your friends to come and visit us and see our excellent display. Now we present the famous artiste, Clara."

Into the ring came a beautiful young lady in a white bathing costume. She climbed up one of the long white ropes hanging down from the top, tied her right hand to the middle of it and started to spin round as she was hanging from it. Hamdah said:

"Doesn't she get dizzy from spinning round?"

"No."

"Why?"

"Because she is very well trained."

'Sawsan Badr' and 'Suhair Ramzi' whispered together as they watched the young lady spinning around, and then laughed heartily. After Clara had come down the assistants brought out a large locker in the shape of a burning house and the clowns came on with a small fire-engine with the bell ringing and halted it by the side of the house. They took off the hose-pipes, spraying the audience with water, and tried to put out the fire, with ridiculous antics. One of them brought a plastic skeleton out of the house. 'Suhair Ramzi's' daughter cried. The clown kissed the skeleton and then slapped it. The dwarf clown then appeared with a water bucket and threw the contents, which turned out to be paper cuttings, over the audience. A girl appeared on the roof of the burning house and stood there calling for help. The clowns brought a ladder to bring her down, but it collapsed. Finally they managed to save her.

The ringmaster repeated his announcement: "We are here for a period of two weeks; come and see us a second time and bring your friends and colleagues with you to visit us. And now, the Nicoli family!"

A young man and a girl entered the ring; the boy was the trainer of the lions and tigers while the girl had an athletic looking body like that of the famous Rumanian gymnast, Nadia Comaneci. The boy began to dance on the tight wire and then he began to skip with a rope on top of the wire. After that, he started to leap over two Italian flags. 'Sawsan Badr' began to bite her nails when she saw him leaping over the flags. The youth then stood on the platform and his sister came and stood on her head on the top of his head. He began to walk along the wire with the extraordinary load on his head while holding, in his right hand, a red sunshade. In the middle of the wire the girl fell off the top of his head. 'Suhair Ramzi' gasped and 'Sawsan Badr' screamed simultaneously.

Nothing happened to the girl because the wire was comparatively close to the ground. The pair made a second attempt and succeeded in completing the full distance along the wire in their extraordinary fashion, to loud clapping from the audience.

Following this act, one of the clowns came into the ring crying. The ringmaster asked him why he was crying, and the clown replied that his lady friend had left and gone to Britain. The ringmaster replied that he must not be sad because in the circus there were many beautiful girls. The clown wandered over to our area and pointed at 'Suhair Ramzi' saying, "I want this beautiful girl." The audience roared with laughter. Then the clown took a rose from the inside of his cloak and went to give it to her, but when she went to take it he pulled it away from her smartly. She laughed and turned to 'Sawsan Badr', bewildered and embarrassed. At that moment the elephant, Dayumu, and its trainer entered the ring. It walked in the ring and then it circled quickly, stopped, raised its right foreleg, then the left one, then the right one again and then the left one. Then it parted its forelegs and sat down on its chest, then it raised both its forelegs high, twice. After that it stood on a little table and began to move as if it were dancing, moving all its legs. Then it got down and sat with its rear end on the table and greeted the audience with its forelegs.

The son of 'Sawsan Badr' quarrelled with the daughter of 'Suhair Ramzi' and then they made up and exchanged sweets. One of the Nicoli brothers entered, stood on his head on the trapeze bar and began to juggle with the rings and the red bows. Hamdah said:

"Why don't the rings fall down?"

"Because he has been coached since he was quite small in how to juggle with them."

"If you begin to coach me now, while I'm small, will I become a circus performer when I grow up?"

I smiled, saying:

"Yes, it's possible that you could become a circus performer."

The ringmaster then announced:

"And now, ladies and gentlemen, the display of the dancing water fountain will commence."

Everything went dark and all eyes were on the fountain at the front of the ring. Music by Wagner came from the recording system, with a dance rhythm, with the water beginning to rise and fall in an exciting fashion, dancing in the coloured lights, green, red and yellow. Everybody was clapping with the music, encouraging the water to twist, bend and dance. The enthusiasm of our German neighbour exceeded that of all others, especially with the playing of the piece *The Ride of the Valkyries,* and even her small daughter was clapping with her.

When we came out of the circus and began to walk towards our car, I asked Hamdah:

"What did you think of the Italian circus?"

She smiled, calmly, and said:

"Nice; not bad!"

WORDS, WORDS, WORDS

That Friday morning Khawla's children had gone off to the beach with their uncle, and, while she was on her way to her mother's house in her new Japanese car, she remembered that she had not brought with her the length of material which she had bought for her mother at the shopping centre the day before. She went back to the house, entering quietly. The length of material was in a bag on top of the television in the small sitting room. She picked it up, and, as she was passing the bedroom door, she heard the voice of her husband coming from the room, saying:

"Don't exaggerate, you idiot!"

She was startled; who was the idiot? Whatever was the idiot talking to her husband about? The door of the bedroom was half-open and she could see, in the wardrobe mirror, her husband stretched out on the bed with the telephone in his hand.

"Listen here, Salim, even with Nadia, who I was desperate for, I never bought presents at that exorbitant price."

" . . . . "

"No, no; Salma, she was something else."

" . . . . "

"I'm demented if I'm in love? Whoever told you that?"

" . . . . "

"Last summer — I didn't go to London, Spain and Cairo chasing Salma. It was pure chance that her family happened to go to the same places that I went to."

" . . . . "

"Why do you laugh and make fun of me when you are worse than I am? Didn't you go chasing after that girl in the red dress to

47

Bangalore, that depressing and boring city, putting up with all the mosquito and insect bites, listening to the prattle of her blind, inane and stupid father?"

" . . . . "

"I agree. My love for that fallen woman was real madness."

" . . . . "

"Yes, I was blind to her shortcomings. I mistook her vulgarity for the signs of being emancipated and modern, and I thought that her stupidity was innocent affection. Her stinginess and materialism were converted, in my eyes, to good economic sense. As for the three lovers she had had before me — she showed me photographs of herself with them — and how her marriage to one of them didn't take place because her father refused to allow it, and how the family of the second one was opposed to his marrying her, and her joking with me that the third one wasn't daring enough for her, all this I interpreted as being due to adolescent thoughtlessness. I told myself that these things happened in the best of families and that our marriage would put an end to them all. Love made me absolutely blind."

" . . . . "

"For sure — the refusal woke me up from those dreams with a shock. For a month in Bombay after the refusal I was drunk and cried and slept with a different woman every night."

" . . . . "

"Sure, ten years, a marriage and children but I'm like an elephant, I don't forget. I still remember her and I still hate her."

" . . . . "

"I know that she was married and divorced."

" . . . . "

"No, her husband didn't catch her with anyone — she's clever. He divorced her because she didn't bear him any children."

" . . . . "

"Yes, I know that, and I know her life is miserable and empty, that she relieves her loneliness by making her body available to anyone."

" . . . . "

"I should feel sorry for her? She can be damned. I'd like to see her completely and utterly destroyed, and if we were living in a country where killers went unpunished then I would kill her myself."

" . . . . "

"You know me well enough; if I love, then it's with intensity, and if I hate, it's also intensely."

" . . . . "

"Moderation is for other situations in life and not for love and hatred. Let's change the subject."

" . . . . "

"My wife, after the first year of marriage, changed from being a wife who was a lover to a mother of children. The period of the giving of presents has ended as far as she is concerned."

" . . . . "

"You hypocrite; all of us, given the chance, would pour kerosene over our wives and burn them."

" . . . . "

"Naturally, any new love is a strong love. Everything Laila says is charming and the ultimate in sweetness; even her lovely chatter about her new dress, and about her quarrel with one of her girl friends, and about the wedding party she went to where she didn't eat anything in order to keep her figure, and about her back tooth which hurts when she eats sweets and which the dentist suggests she has filled, but she is afraid of the pain, and then about her new shoes which she chose with a low heel because when she wears high-heeled shoes she appears taller than her girl friends, and about her finger nails which break off if she lets them grow long..."

" . . . . "

"Yes, you covetous so and so, she tells me everything."

" . . . . "

"We're two of a kind."

" . . . . "

"No, she doesn't mention marriage. She knows just how beautiful she is and the fact that when she wants to marry she will find a lot of gullible men. Don't forget, she's still only eighteen."

" . . . . "

"Me marry her? Just give me the chance."

" . . . . "

"Why do you insist on knowing how much the present cost? Don't forget, we're all the same in this. Didn't you buy the girl in the red dress a gold watch, inlaid with diamonds, which ate into your budget to the tune of 12,000 dirhams?"

" . . . . "

"The English girl is to be pitied. On the contrary, it was she who used to buy me presents, while I used to criticise her for her poor taste. She once bought me a dozen sets of coloured underwear and ten neck-ties. How am I going to wear neck-ties in Dubai?"

" . . . . "

"Yes, she put up with it because she was in love with me. Can you imagine! She wanted to have a child by me without even marrying!"

" . . . . "

"Yes, she said she wanted a permanent memento of me."

" . . . . "

"I don't know, sometimes I think that our love affairs are just to fight boredom."

" . . . . "

"Even with so many available, man always ends up having to make a choice based on his affections. The old kings, they had hundreds, even thousands of concubines, but you'll find that they favoured just one or two."

" . . . . "

"Yes, I had heard that his uncle had died. We all know that our death is somewhere in the near or the distant future, but it's coming, its coming! Sometimes I envy the mentally deranged who are unaware of death."

" . . . . "

"Yes, I'll be at the match today."

" . . . . "

"Cheerio."

After Khawla's husband had put down the handset, he jumped off the bed and went to leave the room. He was surprised to see his wife at the door, standing with her mouth wide open and her eyes staring. He was shocked and said, falteringly:

"You are here! When did you come in?"

She replied, mechanically:

"I was here all the time."

"All the time? You heard all that was said?"

"Yes, all that was said."

Her husband changed his position slightly, then burst into hysterical laughter.

THE SECRET

Al Sayyid Sulaiman Al Ahmar was an eccentric. He wasn't the only remarkable person in Shindagha Quarter, because the area was full of strange and amazing characters, but among these highly individualistic personalities he was, without doubt, outstanding. Sulaiman lived in the western section, near the beach of the Gulf, or the northern sea, and his palm-frond tent was surrounded by a fence of fronds. In the summer, instead of building a shade roof, complete with a *bargeel* to draw down the air, he simply made do with lifting the wind-proof covers of the four walls of his tent to let in some of the light breezes. He was not married and he was not sexually perverted either, and this was odd. He was religious and read the Quran a great deal, as well as other books, the majority of which appeared to be on religious matters.

However, he never went to pray in the mosque, neither during the days of the week nor on Fridays, and not even on feast days; this was also odd. He would use three wire fish traps for fishing and would dive every day to set them down in various places in the Dubai Creek. Every day the traps would fill with fish, not just the fish of the Creek, such as *sha'am* and *saafi*, but appetising and rare fish which had seldom entered the Creek before, for instance the *halwaiyuh*, the *chan'ad*, the *jash* and the *khabaat*, and that was odd too.

He had a white complexion, with a touch of colour; his eyes were grey and had in them an expression difficult to comprehend. He was tall, inclined to be corpulent; his hair was a deep black while his beard was reddish-blond, and that was indeed odd. The people all addressed him as the Sayyid Sulaiman, despite the fact that he was not descended from the family of the Prophet and did not claim to be so descended. Nevertheless, he was in no way disturbed by being addressed by this title, and that was again odd.

He had great affection for young boys and was continually giving them sweets; he used to keep four large glass jars, always full of sweets of various shapes and colours, in his shelter. His great interest in and affection for the small boys had naturally been the source of whisperings and comments, but he showed no concern at all over these matters, which once more was odd.

Through his sweets he was able to attract the attention of the boy Ahmad, son of the fisherman Jasim Humaid. At first, Ahmad would take his sweets from the Sayyid Sulaiman and then go off with his chums, the other boys, but when he noticed that the Sayyid directed his attention towards him in particular, to a greater degree than towards his chums, giving him more sweets, straightening his little skull cap over his long, smooth hair, looking at him penetratingly but compassionately with his grey eyes and always patting him on the shoulder, Ahmad began to prolong his time with him. He would sit at the door of the tent, quietly watching the activities of Sulaiman with great interest.

To begin with, the things that Sulaiman did were practical and, in general, spontaneous, with nothing surprising or startling about them. Within the tent it was almost dark, even in the daytime, and there was a heavy scent of frankincense and myrrh. On the right-hand side was a big wooden bed from India with strange carvings, most of them of serpents and poisonous snakes, with a large bedspread covering it. Beside the bed were two metal chests on which were oil paintings of nature scenes; however, the colours used were very strange. For example, the sky was painted red, the sun was green and the rivers were yellow, while the leaves of the trees were painted on in crimson and the trunks were coloured orange. The two boxes were always locked. The floor of the tent was covered by a mat made of date palm leaves. At the top end of the tent were seven cotton pillows thickly embroidered with hearts and trees. By the side of the bed was a large stand, in the form of two engraved wooden boards, normally used for holding the Holy Quran when reading from it. On the left was the 'corner', or the bathroom, in which was a large closed wooden box and three brass coffee pots, small, medium and large. On the side of the shelter facing the door were three large mirrors, two metres by one metre, which had fine wooden frames with an internal surround, each decorated with four peacocks, one in each of the four corners of the mirrors.

Ahmad's inquisitive eyes would follow the activities of the Sayyid all the time that he was in the tent. Sometimes he would repair his loincloths or his flowing outer garments, while at other times he would work at making the small pipes that locals smoked, using smallish scraps of brown or almost black wood, with bands of silver or brass set in at the mouthpiece, in the middle of the stem of the pipe and at the top of its bowl.

On other occasions he would busy himself with repairing old wire fish-traps or with making some new ones. When he was bending these wires, shaping them or tying them, he would sing in a strange, low tone which reminded Ahmad of the poignant sound of his mother's voice, blended with an attractive huskiness, as she sang the songs and odes of Nabati poetry while doing her dressmaking. He understood only a few words of his mother's singing, despite her clear voice, and he did not understand a single word of the singing of the Sayyid.

The Sayyid did not speak to him much to begin with; rather, he would just throw out a sentence or a clipped question, not usually waiting for an answer but going straight on with his work just as if Ahmad were not even in the tent. Once, when Ahmad was looking, long and hard, at the peacocks surrounding the mirror which was facing him, he heard the voice of the Sayyid saying resolutely:

"The majority of human beings are just like those arrogant birds!"

Ahmad did not understand the meaning of these words, nor why the Sayyid had made this strange comment, and he remained silent, perplexed.

Once, the Sayyid asked him:

"How much of the Quran have you memorised?"

"The Sura of Ya Sin."

"Oh! The very heart of the Quran — who made you memorise it?"

"My mother."

"Do you know the meaning of Ya Sin?"

"No, I don't."

Once, when the Sayyid was stitching up his outer garments, and

Ahmad, with his usual curiosity and detachment, was watching him, he pricked his left thumb with the needle and a couple of drops of blood appeared. He sucked them, continued his stitching and said:

"Do you know where those drops of blood came from?"

"From your thumb."

"Blood always comes from the heart. The heart of man can hold as much love as would make the whole universe happy. It can also carry as much hatred as would destroy creation in its entirety."

Ahmad fell silent in confusion.

Most of Ahmad's visits to the Sayyid were after the '*asr* prayer in the afternoon and ended shortly before darkness fell. The features of the Sayyid's face would change from being tranquil, cheerful and relaxed in the early evening to being depressed and disturbed, but active and animated, as nightfall gently but firmly approached. Ahmad never spoke to anyone about his repeated visits to the tent of the Sayyid.

Once, the Sayyid asked Ahmad:

"What do they teach you in school?"

"Grammar, traditions, Quranic interpretation, arithmetic."

"Is that all?"

"Yes, just those."

"Do you enjoy these subjects?"

"I don't like grammar or arithmetic."

Sometimes the Sayyid would sit cross-legged and read intently from one of the thick tomes opened out on the big stand. His method of reading was a little strange. Sometimes he would remain engrossed in one single page for a long time, perhaps more than an hour, while on other occasions he might look at a page for only one or two minutes. Always, when reading, he would wear a black wool outer garment and twist a red woollen headdress around his head.

Once, the Sayyid was reading from one of his books while Ahmad sat in his usual place, watching him. It was darker than normal inside, and outside, a winter storm was blowing and the tempestuous *shimal* was whistling strangely through the palm fronds. Suddenly, the Sayyid asked:

"Oh, Ahmad — do you know who the masters of the winds and the storms are ?"

"No, Sayyid."

The Sayyid was silent for a time, then he said, in a deep voice with his grey eyes flashing:

"Indeed, they are the tyrants, the evil ones, those who are all powerful, demons, the masters of darkness; their pathways are through the atmosphere, they walk through thick walls, they penetrate the eyes and pass into hearts which they then own as masters own their slaves."

The Sayyid fell silent. Ahmad said in awe:

"Are they the Jinns?"

The Sayyid did not answer Ahmad's question but went on reading. The smell of frankincense became stronger and the forms of its exotic smoke filled the inside of the darkened tent. The Sayyid then said in the same deep tone of voice as before:

"Oh Ahmad — do you know who the overlords of these masters are?"

"No, Sayyid."

The lips of the Sayyid trembled as he continued with his speech while looking at his reflection in a small mirror on the floor in front of him:

"Two groups: first, the group of the pious," (here his voice softened), "those who became rulers in the names of God, who suppressed those who rule by darkness by proclaiming His attributes, thus putting the forces of darkness in dread of Him. Their weapons are complete obedience and total submission to God; with a few inspired words and a firm resolution, the forces of darkness will be led away in humility."

Awe and curiosity filled Ahmad's heart as he asked, almost without thinking:

"And the other group?"

The face of the Sayyid tightened as if it were a sheet of glass and his words came out in a broken and odd fashion:

"The subversive group became the masters of the evil ones of creation and the rebels of the world by ingratiating themselves with them by means of permitting forbidden acts to take place. Their weapons are a total rebellion against the laws of God and a general revolt against His instructions. The forces of darkness are willingly led by them."

That night, before he went to sleep, Ahmad thought a great deal about what the Sayyid had said. To which of the two parties did he belong? Without doubt he belonged to the group of the pious. Was the Sayyid capable of controlling souls and winds? When Ahmad finally went to sleep, he saw himself flying through the air, with the Sayyid holding his hand and flying alongside him, showing him all the four corners of the earth. After that day, the Sayyid never mentioned the subject again, but he had said enough for Ahmad's love and high regard for him to have more than doubled.

Two weeks later Ahmad went to a feast in celebration of the wedding of Fatimah, daughter of Jasim bin Saif, the *Nakhuda*, and he sat with the other boys along the palm frond wall listening to the *Malid*, as the light from the kerosene oil lamps illuminated the party. The bridegroom, his family and the family of the bride were sitting in a single row behind the two lines of the *Malid*; the bridegroom was smiling a great deal. Two young men were going round everyone in the group with the decorative brass pots of bitter coffee and sweet tea, followed by those bearing the incense and rose-water. These were for the men, but a few drops of the rose-water splashed on to Ahmad's face and he felt refreshed by them.

He heard a whisper behind the palm-frond wall; positioning himself close to it, he peeped between the strands of the palm fronds and saw a group of girls who were looking, also through the gaps of the fronds, at the men. He could hear something of what they were saying:

"Look, look — the nose of the bridegroom is so long!"

"His brother, sitting there on his left, is more handsome than he is!"

"You sly so and so, are you hoping that he's going to marry you?"

The girl sighed:

"Would that he were!"

The vocalist of the *Malid* group began to sing, blotting out the girls' whispers:

> *Make my anguish even greater by increasing my love for You*
> *Have mercy on a heart seared by the flame of love for You.*

The sweat was pouring from the vocalist's face as he became totally absorbed in his rendition:

Love is life, die by its power,
By this your death will be vindicated.

The other members of the group were placing their tambourines close to the heaps of red embers on the sand in front of them, and smoothing them out with the bare palms of their hands:

I was perplexed beside his beauty and his splendour,
And the state of affairs itself spoke out for me.

Ahmad was invigorated by the song. When the time came for the meal, all the men and boys rushed forward to the trays and dishes of rice, meat and *harees*. Ahmad didn't join them, as he had already eaten his dinner; he went out, alone, to go home. He walked through some of the dark alleys. He used to be a little afraid of the dark. When he passed the house of the Sayyid, he felt the need to see him, not having done so for two days. However, he had never once visited him at night. He would just greet him and then leave him.

He opened the outside door the way he always did during the daylight hours. The bolt inside was attached to a cord which the visitor would pull from the outside to open the door. It was pitch dark in the compound of the house. Ahmad walked slowly towards the Sayyid's tent. The door was ajar; Ahmad pushed it a little and put his head through it. He froze, nonplussed by fear. The words of greeting died on his lips and he left at a crazy run. He stumbled as his feet hit the threshold of the door, cutting both his feet, but felt nothing. He ran, as if he were flying, to his home.

— 2 —

That night the home of the Sayyid Sulaiman was burnt down. No one came to put out the fire because they were all involved with the wedding feast. Fires, especially in the tents built from palm fronds, were commonplace in those days. But the strange thing was that the fire did not extend to the neighbouring houses; it was as if the fire wanted to confine itself to the house of the Sayyid in order to obliterate it. The following morning, nobody could find anything there except ashes. Everything, the palm fronds, the wood, the clothing, even the metal, had been reduced to ashes. No one knew the fate of the Sayyid. Did he burn with the house or had he just disappeared?

For a long while people made a great fuss about his fate, but eventually the passage of time made them forget about him just as it made them forget many of the other strange events of that quarter. Ahmad lived for another twenty years after the event, living the normal everyday life of a mute.

MY FRIEND

He opened the door of the shop and entered, his red *ghutra* wrapped around his head, with his lean, extraordinary face and small grey eyes and his mouth from which two of his lower front teeth had been lost. I hadn't seen him for a long time, more than three months. Sometimes he would call every day and sometimes every week, while at other times months would pass and I would not see him at all. When he got to my desk he put out his hand and said:

"Give me *zakat*."

I said, smiling:

"This isn't the time for *zakat*."

"Give me the gift for the Feast."

"There are still three months to go for the Feast."

He sat on the chair on the right of the office desk at which I sit and commented:

"I know, I know, the market is stagnant, everybody is complaining about the market; if the market were a woman I would marry her and beat her and withhold any maintenance."

"And where would you get the maintenance to withhold from her?"

"The rain normally falls in the winter but these days it's falling in the summer."

I told the office messenger to bring him some tea and he cried out:

"No sugar, boy!"

"Why?"

"Because nothing does any good with women except beating."

He then took a bundle of notes out of his pocket, Emirates

59

dirhams, Omani riyals and Saudi riyals. He put them on my desk and said:

"Do you know what the benefit of money is?"

"No; what is its benefit?"

"Well, its main benefit is in the buying of locks."

"What are you going to do with this money?"

"Take the lot and give me ten dirhams."

"But it's worth a lot more."

"I want ten dirhams."

"Why?"

"I shall eat rice and *biriyani* in the Indian restaurant and I shall buy a packet of cigarettes."

"But cigarettes are harmful."

"Then why do they sell them?"

"The Ministry of Health warns you about smoking them."

He stood up and went up to the calendar hanging on the wall on the left of my office. On it was the picture of a girl wearing a swimming costume. He whistled loudly and said:

"Sweetmeats are delicious but expensive."

"What have sweetmeats got to do with the girl you are staring at?"

He took a green apple out of the pocket of his black, patched woollen gown, put it on my desk and said:

"Isn't that a lovely orange?"

"But it's an apple, not an orange."

"And I say that it is an orange."

"And I say that it is an apple."

"Who is going to judge between us?"

"Anyone who comes into the shop."

At that very moment Harib, one of my acquaintances, entered the shop. When he saw my friend he smiled and said:

"What's that lunatic doing here?"

My friend stood up. Just as if he had not heard what Harib had said, he rushed up to him to kiss him on the head and say:

"Welcome, welcome to the *nakhuda*, I swear by God Almighty he is the *nakhuda*. Look at the thickness of his *'aqaal*, it really is a *nakhuda's 'aqaal*."

Harib was astonished at my friend's behaviour, and laughed and said:

"When will you get a bit of sanity, you lunatic?"

My friend said, very seriously:

"Are you still living in Sikkit Al Khail ? Your family are all very generous people. Many is the time when I have eaten there through your generosity."

Harib butted in:

"But we live in Jumairah."

My friend went on with what he was saying:

"And that tall date palm in your house. How many times have I climbed it! And that great man, your father!"

Harib commented:

"My father died before I was born."

My friend turned to me and said:

"Do you know what the Municipality is doing?"

I laughed and asked him:

"What is it doing?"

"It's going to impose a tax on everyone who spits in the street, but that doesn't matter to me."

"Why not?"

He smiled and said:

"Because I spit in the Creek."

I told him:

"Sit down and drink your tea."

He began to sip his tea very noisily and then directed the talk to Harib, saying:

"Did you know, *Nakhuda,* that the people in Dubai are mad?"

Harib laughed and said:

"How is that?"

My friend replied:

"They don't know how to live a good life; they get married only once. I say that a man must marry a new woman every year and every woman must get married each year to a new man. If a man were to live for seventy years it would mean that the man had tried and lived the good life with more than fifty women, while similarly a woman would have tried and lived the good life with more than fifty men. This system would make everybody happy."

We laughed at his proposal and asked him:

"Why did you never marry?"

He said, as he looked at the picture of the young girl in the bathing costume:

"These days they play football everywhere, in the houses, in the streets, in the roads and the open spaces."

Harib asked me about the previous evening's football match. When I told him that I hadn't gone, he volunteered to tell me about the highlights of the match and the goals. My friend said, as if he was talking to himself:

"May God curse all seamen — dogs — dogs! Every day, to whichever country they go, they take with them disease and sickness; they are all dogs. All seamen are barking dogs. I do not ask for anything from them but they bark at me ferociously and some of them bite. I swear by God Almighty, some of them bite like mad dogs."

I asked him:

"Why haven't you visited us for such a long time?"

He smiled as he said:

"I was with my girl friend."

Harib laughed and said:

"You! You've got a girl friend?"

"Yes, a sweet girl friend, one with very full buttocks, who goes like this when she walks!"

He got up and walked around the shop in a very funny way. We all laughed, but then his expression suddenly showed him to be ill at ease; he said sadly:

"But her mother is preventing her from seeing me, she doesn't want her to see me. I'll have to kill her mother in order to enjoy the girl."

Harib said:

"You'll become a criminal!"

My friend said:

"From Khan Creek to Al Layya is quite a distance."

Suddenly he turned to me and said.

"Do you know how many cauterisation marks I have on my belly?"

"No."

He took off his *thoub*, and stood there in his loincloth. The scars of the cauterisation burns looked like longitudinal lines on a geographical map. He began to point to them and count:

"One, two, three..."

Harib laughed and said:

"It's as if he has just come out of one of the wars."

When he got to the last burn mark, number fourteen, he said:

"Twenty, the end, and now I want a dirham for each burn mark."

I said with a laugh:

"I'm ready to give you the dirhams, but put your *thoub* on before someone comes into the shop and sees you in this odd state."

My friend was very happy. He put on his *thoub* and sat down to finish his now-cold cup of tea. Beginning to eat the green apple, he said:

"Women are the most delicious thing on earth."

Harib then said, scornfully:

"And what would women want with you?"

My friend laughed and said:

"What would women want from me... ha ha ha... should I tell you what women want from me... ha ha ha... the *nakhuda* doesn't know what women want... ha ha ha ha... is anybody ignorant of what women want?"

I said to my friend as I laughed:

"Which women are the best?"

My friend said, smiling:

"In the winter the black ones are the best because they are warm like a fire, but the white ones are better in the summer because they are cool, like an air-conditioner."

We all laughed and Harib said:

"I wish that I were without worries, like him."

My friend said:

"There are more shops now and the price of goods has increased."

I put the pile of bank notes back in the pocket of his *thoub* and gave him thirty dirhams.

My friend said to Harib, smiling, as he left the shop:

"Women, oh *Nakhuda*, do not forget: women are the most delectable thing in life, women are the most delectable thing in life!"

HABOUBA

The idea of owning a parrot had obsessed Khalifah ever since he had seen, in the house of one of his friends, a parrot which could call him by his name and even insult him. This amused him intensely; after hearing all those insults, one after the other — dog, donkey, pimp, devil — he became fascinated by the parrot. His friend had named it Futoum Kajal. Kajal was Persian for 'bald'.

Futoum the Baldy, in spite of its sharp tongue, loved people caressing it and loved caressing them. When his friend placed it on Khalifah's shoulder, it kissed him on the ear and said, "My darling, my darling, my darling."

Khalifah told his wife he wanted to buy a parrot. She didn't like the idea and showed no enthusiasm. Instead she talked for a long time about prison, bars, freedom, liberty, flying, flight, freedom of movement, seeing the various parts of the world, the different cities, the countless trees, the innumerable houses, seas and rivers, the cruelty of prisons and detention camps, the horror of shackles and imprisonment, the fact that iron shackles and shackles made of gold were all the same, the prisoner's deep hatred of the very eyes of his jailers and his contempt for their faces. Khalifah paid little attention, regarding his wife's comments as idle prattle. He was used to the chatter of his wife, and he was also used to ignoring it.

— 2 —

Khalifah made repeated visits to his friend, the owner of the parrot Futoum Kajal, and whenever it insulted him, then kissed him and said to him, "My darling, my darling, my darling," his envy and his fascination with the parrot increased, as did his determination to purchase one like it. He listened to an absolute flood of information and guidance from his friend about buying a parrot:

"Futoum Kajal is an African parrot of the Kaskoo species...

"Kaskoo is the best species of parrot in the world...

"No parrot on earth can utter the speech of man, in all its different tones, enunciating the words absolutely clearly, like a Kaskoo can...

"The Kaskoo parrot is known to live for a long time, as long as seventy-five years."

Khalifah was amazed by all this information. It meant that if he bought a young Kaskoo parrot, about two or three years old, it would live on after his death and be inherited by his children and his wife. He wondered which of them would ask for the parrot as part of his share of the inheritance. He laughed at the idea and went on listening to his friend.

"Most of the Kaskoo parrots in the bird shops in Dubai and Sharjah are too troublesome; they scream a lot and try to bite anyone who tries to pet them."

"The Kaskoo is like all other parrots; it likes to be petted by people by being stroked on the head and neck, but it very strongly dislikes anyone stroking it on the tail." Khalifah laughed.

"I used to have a very nice, mild-mannered and intelligent parrot whose name was Soraya. My father came to visit me, and he knew nothing about the handling of parrots. He was very pleased because she called him by name, and he began to stroke her quite heavy-handedly on the tail, thinking that he was petting her. The parrot attacked him and bit his fingers so badly that they bled. He grabbed it angrily by its legs and smashed it against the wall three times, as a result of which it died." Khalifah laughed again.

"Female parrots, generally speaking, have an aversion towards women and avoid contact with them. My parrot Soraya didn't like women, and if my mother or any of my sisters came and tried to pet her, she would become very uneasy and would scream and not do anything for them. But if any of my brothers or pals came she would be very relaxed. She would whistle and talk, address them by their names and kiss them, and be delighted by their petting."

— 3 —

Khalifah passed on all this information to his wife, adding little anecdotes and embellishments of his own in order to endear his wife to the idea of their owning a Kaskoo parrot. Gradually the wife began to accept the prospect and began to talk about how from childhood she had loved animals and birds. She said that her sister had owned a white cat with an orange patch on its back, while her brother used to have a black dog called Antar, a nice dog which had played with her and her brother and had lived in her family's house for many years. Her mother, too, used to look after a lot of animals, and she particularly remembered a large brown cow which was her mother's pride and joy. She used to call it the *'Mabrooka'* because its milk was the finest, while its butter would fill a small jar. She also had numerous birds, including hens and ducks. Her father used to keep two canaries, yellow and green in colour, in the sitting room, and just looking at them would make him relax.

Khalifah didn't pay much attention to the prattle of his wife, but he was pleased that her chatter indicated that she approved of the idea of owning their own Kaskoo parrot. Khalifah decided that he was going to buy the parrot. He went with his friend to the places selling birds, but they were unable to find easily what they so badly wanted. Bird Paradise had every species of parrot — except Kaskoo parrots. Happy Birds had Kaskoos but they were a troublesome lot and screamed abominably. Dream Birds had four Kaskoos, but they were all savage and would bite anyone. The one Kaskoo parrot that Dubai Aviaries had was quiet and sensible, but its price was unreasonable: 3,000 dirhams. (Khalifah's friend whispered in his ear that the place was a den of thieves and that the price of the best Kaskoos never exceeded 1,500 dirhams under any circumstances.)

Beauty Birds did have three Kaskoos, but they were still young chicks and their feathers had not yet sprouted on their necks and bodies. (Khalifah's friend whispered again into his ear that he shouldn't buy from them because the parrot might die while it was still growing up and, who knows, it might even have some sickness or other. Anyway, its form did not inspire confidence.) Animal World had four Kaskoos which were well behaved and nicely formed (but here again his friend whispered to him, cautioning him against buying, for their feathers were mainly black, and the black Kaskoo parrots were more dull-witted than the greys and did not learn as easily or as quickly).

For a week, Khalifah and his friend continued to visit the bird and animal establishments in both Dubai and Sharjah, but to no avail, for there was no trace of a pure-bred grey Kaskoo parrot which was well-behaved, obedient and trained. In the end, Khalifah became weary, but his friend promised him that he would continue his efforts in the search to find the rare bird. Khalifah told his wife about all the difficulties of finding a suitable parrot. She was amazed by all this, as she had thought it would be a simple matter; there were many establishments selling birds, all full of cages of parrots and decorative birds.

After a week, Khalifah's friend came with a look of triumph on his face. He had found the required Kaskoo. It wasn't cheap, but it wasn't too expensive either: 1,100 dirhams. It was well-behaved and didn't scream, but would need training. He undertook to train it for Khalifah for a month and a half. Khalifah agreed, gratefully, both to the price and to leaving the parrot with his friend for training for a period of forty-five days.

Khalifah passed on the good news to his wife. She was delighted but a little irritated about the matter of the parrot staying with his friend. Khalifah tried to placate her on the soundness of the move by telling her that his friend understood the psychology of birds and that he knew when to deprive them of food and when to feed them in order to train them and teach them to speak.

She laughed at his explanation and said that the use of the starvation and feeding method for teaching birds and animals was not the invention of his friend. She remembered reading about it in a schoolbook on psychology in which a Russian scientist would starve his dogs in order to study their behaviour and teach them certain tricks.

Khalifah wasn't very pleased with his wife's criticism; however, while they were waiting for the parrot, they made preparations in a state of anticipation, busying themselves with every detail. The parrot was a female; what would they call it? They thought of a number of names: Fairouz, Habouba, Co-co, Tayyara, Jamila, Lulu,

Zahour, Falwa, Kouthr, Malika, Asmahan. Should they keep it in a cage or should they use a metal perch without a cage? Khalifah wanted the cage but his wife insisted on the metal perch. All right, where would they put the cage or the metal perch? In the kitchen, in the hall, in the sitting room or on the verandah? Khalifah wanted it to be near the kitchen because he frequently went in there. His wife wanted it on the verandah near the henna bush because it was closer to nature. What would they feed it? Khalifah said that his friend had told him that it would eat seed and fruit and everything. His wife said that there must be a special food for it which would be more beneficial than any other. Then Khalifah suddenly got a cold. He asked, as he was taking the medicine his wife had prepared for him, what they would do if the parrot took sick. His wife reassured him that there was an old English veterinary surgeon in Jumairah who treated animals, birds and domestic pets.

Every day Khalifah would get in touch with his friend to ask about his parrot. What had it learnt? Did it enunciate its words clearly? Was it quick or slow? Did it detest women and girls like other Kaskoo parrots? Did it eat with a good appetite after training? Khalifah's friend would continually reassure him about the positive response of his parrot to the training programme.

— 4 —

After a month, Khalifah went to visit his friend to see his parrot. He had not seen it since the day of its purchase. He was longing to have the grey bird with the red tail; he was delighted when he heard it call him by his name. His friend took it out of the cage and handed it to him. Khalifah set it on three fingers of his right hand and held it up to his face. It kissed him on his ear and on his cheek and called out, "My darling, my darling, my darling." Khalifah was delighted and enjoyed the kisses and calls immensely. They reminded him of his cousin Iman who, when they were little children, about eight years of age, would kiss him on the cheek and say to him, "You are my darling, you are my husband."

Khalifah wanted to take the parrot home there and then, but his friend stopped him, gently but firmly insisting that it was necessary for it to remain with him for another ten days in order for him to complete the training. Khalifah agreed reluctantly.

He went home, full of enthusiasm. He told his wife about the emotive kisses and calls. They agreed to settle all the troublesome decisions before the parrot's arrival. They chose the name of Habouba for it, and they bought both a cage and a metal perch. In the winter they would put it in the cage and in the summer they would put it on the perch. It would be kept near the big almond tree between the verandah and the kitchen, and the feed would be of a specific type consisting of seeds and apple. Khalifah said to his wife, jokingly:

"If it shuns you, then wear a man's outer garment and put on a false beard."

That night they saw a television programme about the various types of African parrots. The Kaskoo was among the many parrots of different sizes and colours with their strange voices and characteristics.

There were only two days left before Habouba's arrival at her new home with Khalifah and his wife. Everything was ready: the cage, the perch and the seeds and apples. The telephone rang and the wife picked it up. She passed on the good news to Khalifah:

"It's your friend."

Khalifah took the hand-set quickly and spoke to his friend. After a few seconds the look on his face froze. He put the hand-set down and said to his wife, hesitantly:

"My friend says that when Habouba's cage was on the floor, she began to scream and shout at his demented black cock. It attacked her and pecked her eyes out."

A RAINY NIGHT

isha had been a strong woman, but two stages of her life had conspired against her to lead to her being prostrate in a large bed in a Bombay hospital. The first stage was fifty years of poverty. When she was just a child, she had helped her aunt who sold fish. She had married an absentee husband, the *nakhuda* of a *boom*, who would return to Dubai and make her pregnant and then disappear for many months, moving like a phantom between the Gulf ports and the Arabian sea, visiting Bandar Abbas, Gwadar, Aden, Mombasa, Bahrain, Kuwait and other places. The wives of other *nakhudas* lived a comparatively luxurious life, but Aisha's life was very hard. Her husband, on the few occasions when he returned to Dubai, was very tight-fisted towards her. She heard from one of her relatives that he was supporting a number of other wives in Bandar Abbas, Bahrain and Mombasa, and a neighbour told her that his money was reserved for drink and ladies of pleasure. Her hard life did not permit her the luxury of jealousy or the satisfaction of complaint. Her sole care was her five children, three boys and two girls.

Many years went by as she toiled continually to feed the five mouths and bring a smile to the children's faces. At the end of those years she suffered from the effects: emaciation, poor sight, bowed legs, the loss of her teeth and... and... and... and...

The second stage was twenty years of affluence and the enjoyment of spending money. Aisha's father died at the end of the 1960s and her share of the inheritance was a large piece of land on the Dubai side of the Creek, which was sold for three million dirhams. In addition, all three of her sons were in prosperous circumstances. The eldest had become a cement dealer and builder's merchant. The second son became rich from the presents and commission which he received by virtue of his work with the government, where he became an important official and a highly-respected director. The third son had opened a small shop near the charcoal market and joined the ranks of the well-known and successful, although the source of the wealth was not known exactly. He said that he traded with Iran and Pakistan, but some of the witty drunkards would remark, during their evening sessions, that the wealth was from trading in fine opium, refreshing cocaine and enjoyable *hasheesh*. However, all this was just unconfirmed gossip, for the third son could be seen in his gold-embroidered *bisht* at all the big parties and solemn funerals, and no cases had ever been brought against him in the courts. Indeed, in his whole lifetime he had only ever actually been in the court building once. Aisha's elder daughter had never married and still lived with her, while the younger daughter had married the partner of her eldest brother and had produced half a dozen children.

During those twenty years, Aisha took her revenge on the poverty, degradation and hunger of the previous long years. She built a big house for herself in Jumairah with more than ten large rooms. She competed with the young girls in the clothing she wore, the embroidered silk dresses and golden jewellery, embellished with diamonds, sapphires, emeralds and rubies. She would sleep for long periods. She bought three cars, a Mercedes for her own use, a Toyota for the kitchen requirements and a Range Rover for desert trips.

But the main arena for her revenge was food. She always thought of those bitter days when if she had taken lunch then she couldn't have dinner; if her children, with their hunger, sat down to the fish, then all that would be left for her would be the gravy. She would never miss a single wedding party just so she could take home some food afterwards to her children, putting it into a cooking pot which she carried with her; she would also put fruit in her pockets.

Prosperity allowed Aisha to indulge herself with a very rich diet. In the morning she would prepare for herself, according to the season, various well-known types of bread. In winter she would have a loaf of the thick, *Al Khameer*, covered with a coating of eggs and sesame, and a loaf of *Al Jabaab*, covered with eggs and dipped in local butter. With this loaf she would eat butter whipped with honey, various cheeses and eggs cooked with tomatoes. In addition to these loaves, there would be other delicacies for the breakfast table such as *Al Balaleet* — pasta cooked with sugar and topped with a round flat loaf made from eggs — and a pie, sometimes made up from thin unleavened bread and sugar and sometimes from pulped pumpkin and sugar, which Aisha wouldn't touch until she had poured over it a dreadful amount of the local *ghee*. There was *Al Khabeesa*, made from thin, unleavened bread and sugar, which Aisha did not like unless she had sprinkled it with several large spoonfuls of extra sugar. *Al Hareesah* also had to be on the breakfast table every morning. This was ostentatiously excessive, because even in the houses of the very rich, the paste of *hareesah*, made from meat and whole wheat, is made only during the days of Ramadan and feast days and on the occasion of weddings, circumcisions and the birthday of the Prophet. However, it pleased Aisha to see the big plate of *hareesah* every morning, because it reminded her, in particular, of a relative of hers who was married to one of the merchants during her years of poverty, who would enjoy *hareesah* very often, both during Ramadan and at other times, never sending any, however, to Aisha, except on one or two occasions during Ramadan. Now Aisha could savour *hareesah* every day. The shape of the big dish of thick *hareesah*, covered with *ghee*, was a welcome sight to her eyes and cheered her up. In addition to these dishes, Aisha still had an appetite for some of the things which she used to enjoy during the period of poverty, such as beans in summer and chick peas in winter, and sometimes molasses.

The lunches and dinners were sumptuous meals; there would be fish, fried and grilled (she used to refer to the fish as "the fruit of the sea"), fish broth or meat broth, *thuraid*, with chicken or with meat, *kababs* of meat, chicken or fish, and white rice or sweet reddened rice, spread either above or below the main part of the dish, with spices, garlic, onion and lemon. Because of her love of variety she would sometimes eat different types of dried fish, such as *yowbal* and *jaseef*, and salted fish. A new set of false teeth helped her chew all this.

Visits from her lady friends had to be punctuated by the offering of various kinds of fruit, Omani sweetmeats, both red and black, *rahash*, a floury sweetmeat, biscuits, and Damacus sweetmeats, chocolates, cakes and a Western gateau. As for milk and other dairy produce, she did not buy them from a shop but set up a compound outside her house in which were four cows to provide all the yoghurt, milk, buttermilk, dried yoghurt and *ghee* which was consumed in the house. When she sat up at night with her daughter in front of the television, it was inevitable that she would finish off a whole jug of milk, accompanied by some biscuits. She substitued the enjoyment of food for all the joys of marriage, love, motherhood and children. The loaf of *khameer*, saturated in *ghee*, full of honey and butter, brought to her mouth untold delight. The *ghee*, as it was poured from a large cup on to a plate of white rice, brought to her nostrils a fragrant and intoxicating scent, while the Omani sweetmeats, when presented to her, fresh and warm, were a sight which surpassed that of the most beautiful flowers, including roses, in the world.

Over the previous five years, Aisha had reached ninety kilograms, and, in addition to the results of the years of hunger, she now had the results of the years of plenty: diabetes, high blood pressure, kidney problems, rheumatism, varicose veins, diseases of the stomach and the liver, difficulties with the heart, asthma and problems with the lungs. She had reached a state in which she was taking, in any one day, thirty pills of various kinds. All the recommendations of the doctors that she should lose weight failed to penetrate the barrier of her well-known phrase, which she continually repeated: "If I do not eat I shall die."

— 2 —

In Aisha's private room in the Bombay hospital, the three brothers, the two sisters and the husband of the younger girl sat on wooden and metal chairs, drinking tea and eating biscuits which they had brought with them, while being looked after by the two nurses. The first of these was a skinny Hindu who wore a medallion around her throat on which was the likeness of the elephant god, Ganesh; the second was a well-built Christian who wore a small gold cross around her neck. They knew that these were their mother's final days, but she rarely came into their conversation. The eldest brother was involved in a continuous argument with his partner, the husband of his sister, about sacking the company's Indian accountant, whom they had recently appointed after the death of the previous Pakistani accountant who had served them loyally for two decades. The sister's husband was trying to give him more time to prove his loyalty and trustworthiness, while the elder brother insisted that he was a crook because of his gleaming eyes and sharp and vicious comments. He felt sure that the bright accountant was an experienced thief and member of the criminal world.

The other two sons, the second and the third, were talking about the perpetual rainy weather in Bombay during the summer. The second son said:

"If we had this rain in Dubai, our city would drown and us with it, and the city would probably be swept away to form an island, floating in the Gulf."

The third recollected the storm of 1957 which struck Dubai with great violence and force. The small boats in the Creek were destroyed, a big ship was blown from the Creek to one of the residential areas and houses collapsed onto the heads of their occupiers and killed them. Tents made from date palms caved in or were uprooted from their foundations; dogs, cats, and lambs flew through the air, and the tempestuous wind smashed the bodies of seagulls and pigeons against the walls of the stone houses and strong date-palm tents which had survived the blast.

The two sisters were discussing the children of the younger sister. The mother was very concerned about her son Khalid, who was studying in America; he had married without informing her. His uncle, who had visited America recently to check up on his own sons who were studying in the same state, had informed her about the marriage, telling her:

"The American woman that Khalid has married has four children from a previous marriage; the oldest is fifteen and has a black belt in karate."

Her daughter, Wadad, had completed secondary school but had not gone on to university; she slept all day, visited the markets from afternoon to sunset and then made telephone calls until almost dawn. The elder daughter said that what Wadad needed was a husband. Her sister laughed and said:

"I know that, but nobody has come forward for her yet; what do I do? Do I put an advertisement in the papers asking for a husband for her or do I put a notice on the back of her cloak saying: 'Wanted: ox for this cow'?"

Aisha was unaware of all these conversations. Sometimes she would talk deliriously, in just broken words and sentences:

"...the cows... who... will feed them... today, I'm going to get married... no... no, don't let my husband come in... I want to put my perfume on... do my make-up... cold... it's all very cold... cold... cold... cold... very... sweetheart... oh sweetheart... oh sweetheart... where is the watch... the diamond one... I want to wear it... I want to have my henna put on... bring the henna... don't put too much dried lemon in it... bring on the drums... bring on the dancers... the black cow is in calf... don't let her calve... the father will come... the great ox... he eats his young... the sheep eats its young... the dog eats its young... the fathers eat their sons... the bed hurts me... I need a cotton pillow... I should have the bride's bed... I am a bride... bring the car... I want to go to the house... I want to go to the market... the cows are in the market... they are going to beat my dear cows... the municipality is going to seize my cows and hurt them... in that big compound... the municipality is criminal... my sweetheart is going to flog the municipality and teach it a lesson... be quiet... be quiet... my sweetheart is asleep... my husband is asleep... do not disturb him... do not wake him up... he is tired... very tired... very, very tired... the night is long... these days are very long... the daytime is short... we have breakfast... then a minute later we have lunch... after dinner... the night is long... very long... a husband shortens the long... . night... yesterday... white teeth appeared for me... new... fresh.... small... like milk teeth..."

Her children, hearing these words and sentences, smiled. Some of them laughed, and they then continued their conversations.

— 3 —

On the Tuesday night, they came early in order to leave early. It was raining heavily, unceasingly, and umbrellas were of no use. The streets of the city were full of children and disabled beggars. At half-past seven they had wanted to leave, but Aisha gave them a weak signal that she wanted them to stay with her. She whispered a few words which she clearly had great difficulty in uttering:

"... take me... to the house... I'm afraid... from India... I'm afraid of the heat... it's so hot... unbearably hot... my husband is waiting for me... who... will prepare... his dinner... the henna... black... in... my hand... black... like... night..."

The children remained in their mother's room, talking about the heavy rain outside. The elder brother asked his sisters if they had bought a perfume spray of oil of frankincense. One of them answered that it was more expensive than gold and that most of it was adulterated and mixed with alcohol; it therefore burnt with a flame, unlike the pure oil of frankincense which did not flame. The younger daughter asked her husband for more money; she had already bought presents for some of her relatives, but had not bought presents for her husband's sisters and her friends and did not want to go back empty-handed, especially as this was her first visit to Bombay. There were many attractive things which she had noticed while strolling around the markets with her sister. The youngest brother said that on the previous evening he had attended the wedding of Haji Khalifah Khalfan to a young Indian girl. The elder sister was astonished and said disapprovingly:

"Khalifah Khalfan is older than my mother; there is no doubt that he is out of his mind. This sort of behaviour is one of the signs of senility and old age. Such lunacy! Tomorrow the girl will be pregnant and they'll say that it's his offspring, and then that senile old man will take the baby around his elderly friends and all the old women of the family to prove that he is still like a billy-goat."

The eldest son said:

"They say that our father was married in the port of Bandar Abbas; where are our brothers and sisters?"

The youngest brother laughed and said:

"Your brothers are porters on the quays of the port, while your sisters are ladies of the street in one of its quarters."

His elder sister cursed him as she laughed. The eldest son told his partner that he had interviewed several Indian accountants for the post with them in Dubai. He had found only one of them satisfactory, one who gave the appearance of being a harmless, trustworthy old man. He had asked him to come the following morning so that he could introduce him to his partner. They discussed the increase in prices; the elder sister remarked that this was one of the signs of the approach of doomsday. The younger brother commented that wages and salaries had also increased. They criticised the highly-spiced Indian food at the hotel, its inferior service and the lobbies and corridors which gave off an odour of kerosene and were full of cockroaches. The eldest son commented that in Dubai, for the same price, they could live in a luxury hotel with the odours of scented soap emanating from the rooms. The second son said that he had had a dream the previous night in which he saw his son Hamad, who had died two years earlier, riding on the back of a horse and wearing an embroidered frock; all of his teeth were gold. Although he called Hamad several times by his name, he failed to respond; however, he turned before disappearing with his horse and said to him,

"My name is Fatimah, not Hamad."

The elder daughter explained the meaning of the dream as being that her brother's wife, who was pregnant, would give birth to a girl and that they must name her Fatimah. The younger daughter then said that she had had a short, strange dream while in Bombay, in which she saw her six children in the form of six small green birds carrying locks of various shapes and sizes in their beaks. The elder daughter said that the children of her sister loved travel and that they respected their mother. They talked together for a long time on the interpretation of dreams.

At ten o'clock, the five children stood up, kissed the brow of their sleeping mother and left.

— 4 —

At three o'clock in the morning, the eldest brother was awakened by the telephone ringing. When he took the handset, the doctor supervising his mother's treatment said that he was sorry to disturb him at that late hour of the night, but thought that his mother was now approaching death. Leaving his room in the hotel, he quickly awakened a taxi driver sleeping in his taxi near the hotel. A quarter of an hour later he was in his mother's room.

By her side was the Christian nurse and the lean doctor, who said to him that her breathing was very weak and that it was likely that these were her last few minutes. The eldest brother sat on a metal chair alongside the bed. He looked at the face of his mother; the eyes had become sunken and the nose shrivelled and crooked. Her mouth was empty of teeth and her sallow, flabby skin full of spots.

He stayed by her side for half an hour, listening to her breathing, which was gradually becoming shallower. He asked the nurse to bring a glass of water. After he had drunk it, he could no longer hear his mother's breathing. He called the doctor and said to him:

"I think she has died."

An hour later he was in a taxi on his way back to the hotel. The rain was still pouring down in torrents, but he could see the drivers of the bullock-carts and hordes of labourers and employees going off early to their work: some were walking, some were running, and some were hobbling.

LIFE IS GIVEN AND
LIFE IS TAKEN AWAY

hen 'Ashok Mehta mounted the camel he was ill at ease. It was the first time in his life that he had ridden a camel, but he had to leave Dubai for Abu Dhabi and the camel was the only means of transport available. The beduin leading the camel had asked for five rupees for the journey, a large sum to which 'Ashok had reluctantly agreed.

One of the relatives of his neighbour, who had recently arrived in Dubai from Bombay, had told him that two men had arrived there from his home village looking for him. 'Ashok was alarmed. He remembered the incident which had caused him to run away from his village. He hadn't intended to kill that young man. It was true that 'Ashok's physique was clearly strong but he was in fact a great coward. When he had grabbed the youth he was only playing with him. He had gently pressed on his throat. The lad was laughing and then, after a little while, his laughter suddenly froze on his face. When 'Ashok realised that he was dead he didn't wait to explain to his family what had happened. Overcome by fear, he fled to Bombay.

He lived for a full year in that city, but disliked it. He worked as a stevedore in the port and he sold fruit by the side of one of the cinemas but his fear remained with him. In Bombay he bought a steamship ticket from his savings. He had wanted to go to East Africa but luck took him to Dubai. Now, fear was driving him to Abu Dhabi.

— 2 —

The camel went along parallel to the beach, the beduin walking in front. From time to time he would turn around, look at 'Ashok, shake his head and grin. His teeth were pure white and his eyes were placid, while his face had harsh features, scorched by the sun. Three hours of travel and they had met nobody. After they had passed the last inhabited settlement, Umm Al Suqaim, they had a rest. Later they stopped for a second time near Khor Ghanadha. When 'Ashok dismounted the beduin attacked him and tied him up with a rope which he had kept wound around his waist. 'Ashok went rigid and was unable to defend himself. When he saw the beduin pull out his knife he wet his trousers with fright. It was a long knife of the type with the blade concealed in the handle. The beduin tried to pull the blade out and failed. He tried again. He tried a third time but without any luck. Sweat poured from him and his smile disappeared. The fourth time he used all his strength and pulled at the blade as hard as he could. The blade came out with a jerk and he overbalanced, the blade passing across his throat, slitting it from ear to ear. The beduin fell, shuddering. Bleeding profusely, he drew his last breath. Fear and bewilderment almost caused 'Ashok to die too.

— 3 —

Khalifah Salim and his three sons were returning to Dubai from Abu Dhabi in their old boat. They had wanted to sell it there, but had been unable to find a buyer. Hassan, Khalifa's youngest son, had tried to catch a fish for lunch but without success, despite the fact that the area was a well-known spot for bottom-fishing, with plenty of fish. As they were approaching Khor Ghanadha, a *chanaad* leaped up and into their boat. They were overjoyed and went ashore to collect firewood to grill the fish, their guest. There they found 'Ashok, tied up, and the dead beduin. The sight was astonishing but self-explanatory. When they returned with 'Ashok, now totally confused, and the firewood, the *chanaad* leaped out of the boat into the creek and disappeared into the deep.

THEY'LL KILL YOU

he looked at him in fear and surprise as she wiped the sleep from her eyes, and said in astonishment:

"What brought you here?"

He pushed open the door and came in, looking at her bitterly. She was wearing a white gossamer gown which displayed her throat and a fair area of her breast:

"I came to see you."

She sat down on the large wooden bed and he sat on one of the cushions at the top end of the palm-frond tent, resting on his rifle. She said:

"They'll kill you!"

He didn't answer. It was spring, and the rays of the moon, which was at its brightest, filtered between the palm fronds of the room so that the interior was quite visible, just as if it were early morning. Habiba's tent was outside the walls of Deira, which extended from the square watchtower at Al Khakak to the sea of the Gulf in the north, then to the watchtower of Hashar by the sea at the Creek. Inside the wall was the residential area of the Deira people, protected by guards, while outside the wall were the scattered tents of groups of foreigners, such as gypsies, prostitutes, petty artisans and other outsiders. These tents were protected by the heavens.

Salim looked at Habiba as she sat high up on the large wooden bed; her two smooth legs dangled down, but they couldn't touch the ground because she was so short.

Her bright but indolent look, her body, which was rounded in all the right places, the long locks of her hair, scattered around untidily on her breast and on her shoulders, and her two, dark, bright eyes

83

made her look like some Eastern priestess who would bewitch anyone on whom her gaze might fall.

He said, with a note of sadness in his voice:

"Aren't you going to get me... any coffee?"

Coffee in the middle of the night, she said to herself, he must be mad.

She got down off the bed and went to the corner of the tent, lit the charcoal fire and began to get the coffee pot ready.

— 2 —

The first time she had seen him had been in the market at Dubai. Salim had come to sell a camel which he had stolen from one of the caravans. She saw the large amount of money that he was tying up in his loin-cloth and was captivated by the sight of the silver riyals. She spoke to him, then invited him to have lunch with her in her home. She gave him lunch, and pleasured him. He gave her all the money from the sale of the stolen camel. From that day on, he became more audacious in his pillaging, whether with his gang or on his own. Although he was well aware that she was a prostitute and a lady of pleasure, he nevertheless loved her, and his love for her drove him to act insanely.

— 3 —

Habiba had many visitors, the main one being the merchant and pearl dealer, Ali Sulaiman, who was infatuated with her and spent money on her incessantly. Indeed, he would give her many valuable gifts, including an expensive gold necklace, which she kept in a little wooden box hidden in a hole in the ground under the large bed. He would also give money to obscure poets to compose odes praising the beauty and figure of Habiba. Once, during an evening party the poet Khamis Riyaan recited a poem of ten verses in which he described Habiba. When he reached the verse where he said: "Her teeth are like perfectly shaped pearls, the fragrance of her breath is as musk and perfume," Ali Sulaiman leapt to his feet, pulled out five silver riyals, and gave them to the poet. Habiba made a pretence of being flattered by the incident, but quietly wished that it had been her who had received the five silver riyals.

— 4 —

When she formed the relationship with Salim, Ali Sulaiman was on a long trip to Bombay, lasting for five months. On the very day he returned, after he had greeted his family and his agents, his heart led him to the tent of Habiba who welcomed him and the many gifts which he had brought from India for her. She was childishly happy with the *fatkh*, the large, gold rings which a woman would wear on each of their big toes, so that when she walked in the tent they would produce a jingling sound.

As luck would have it, Salim came to her tent that very night. When he heard the laughter coming from inside, his heart stopped. He didn't enter the tent. He listened cautiously to the noises inside, and when it became clear to him what was going on, his heart broke. He bit his lower lip until the blood ran. His eyes filled with tears, in spite of himself, and the tears flowed, mixing with the blood from his lip. Love and hatred rooted him to the outside corner of the tent.

Just before dawn Ali Sulaiman came out of Habiba's tent. Salim wanted to shoot him, there and then, but was afraid that the guards would hear him. He unsheathed his broad-bladed *khanjar* and buried it in the chest of Ali Sulaiman, who let out a loud scream that brought some of the gypsies running from their tents. Salim escaped in the pitch darkness.

— 5 —

Ali Sulaiman's family wanted to kill some of the gypsies out of revenge but were unable to prove anything against them. There was a lot of talk. Habiba became very afraid and very nearly fled to another city. But suddenly the talking died down.

— 6 —

After Salim had drunk the first cup of coffee, he looked into Habiba's eyes. They were not as seductive or as sensuous as before. Indeed, her face reflected a mixture of alarm, sadness, dejection and fear.

She said again in an agitated tone:

"They'll kill you!"

He gave no indication that he had heard her. He stood up, rigidly, and led her, shaking with terror, to the large bed.

— 7 —

When he came out of the entrance there was the sound of a shot. The bullet went through Salim's chest, and he dropped at the door of the tent.

JUST STANDING THERE, SMILING

aqar arrived back home, exhausted. When he entered the courtyard of the house he called out to his wife:

"Bring me the rifle."

His wife said, in a frightened voice:

"Why?"

He went on shouting:

"I'm going to kill that wicked ape."

His wife asked:

"What has she done this time?"

He sat down and began to wipe the perspiration from his brow, and the ape joined him in wiping it up. He struck it with his hand and laughed bitterly:

"Oh, you shameless hussy, do you want them to put me in prison?"

The ape went off into a corner and acted as though she were angry. Saqar went on talking:

"As usual, I tied her up to the leg of the big bench outside the shop. When I came out and didn't find her, I thought that she might be wandering around the back streets and would return to the shop before nine o'clock when I close up. I waited until ten o'clock and, just as I was beginning to lose hope of her coming back, the telephone rang. It was one of my friends, a police officer, telling me to come to the police station in order to collect this stupid ape."

His wife said:

"And what had Umm Kamil done?"

He replied, angrily:

"She isn't Umm Kamil, she is a felon and a lunatic. After slipping her chain, she sneaked through the alleys and lanes and the streets and then went into the Hyatt Regency Hotel and got as far as the reception hall, the one where they hold big parties, and there was a large wedding party going on. Can you imagine the confusion at the party as a result of Umm Kamil, the beast, honouring it with her presence?"

In spite of the fact that Saqar's wife sympathised with him, she was unable to stop herself from smiling. Her husband said:

"Go on, laugh. Just think if it had been the wedding of one of your sisters or daughters! The first thing that she went for was the big wedding cake. She toppled it over and then trampled on it. After the bridegroom's headdress had fallen off, he fled, leaving behind his fine *bisht*. The bride froze on the spot from fear. Then Umm Kamil went and sat in the groom's chair, took the bride's veil off her head and put it on her own. The women and children were screaming louder and louder. The waiters, the members of the band and the families of the bride and groom all tried to catch hold of her, but she turned the reception hall into a circus. She would begin to taunt them and then run away, over and under the tables, grabbing the women's cloaks and throwing plates of food and glasses of drinks all over them. Finally, a large squad of police managed to catch hold of her. By the grace of God, the officer at the police station turned out to be a good friend of mine; if he had been someone who didn't know me, I would have finished up in court with a big case."

His wife said, as she laughed:

"But Umm Kamil is an entertaining creature."

— 2 —

Saqar and his wife loved animals. They had goats, ducks, a tortoise, a parrot, dogs and cats. A year before all this, Saqar, his wife and small son had been going around the pet-shops. They saw a large chimpanzee eating nuts. The owner of the shop had put a blue and white sailor's cap on its head and a red scarf around its neck. The ape shook hands with Saqar's son, who liked her and was adamant that his father should buy her. When the father asked the cost of the ape, the shop owner told him that it was 5,000 dirhams. The father backed off when he heard such a high price, but the cries and tears of his son, together with the begging and pleading of his wife, forced him to buy the ape, which his wife named Umm Kamil.

The troubles began from the time Umm Kamil arrived at the house. On her second day there, she managed to sneak on to the roof of the neighbours' house, open the water cistern and take a refreshing bath on the hot summer's day. It cost Saqar dearly for the playful ape's bath, as he had to buy a new water cistern for the neighbours, and pay to have it fitted, to replace the one befouled by Umm Kamil.

As far as the grocer next to the house was concerned, Umm Kamil became a perpetual terror, for whenever she managed to free herself from her wooden cage or from the chain with which they used to tie her to the big almond tree, she would automatically go off to the grocery. As soon as she had entered the shop, his customers would scatter; he himself would stand rigidly in his place, while the ape would open the refrigerator and throw all the bottles and tins of soft drinks in it on the floor, eat some cheese, slide along the shelves and throw most of the tins of foodstuffs, children's toys and soap on to the floor. Then she would choose a kind of biscuit which Saqar's son particularly liked, and leave, accompanied by the curses of the owner of the shop. He would then rush to assess his losses after her attack and register these losses on the account of Saqar, who would pay the extra each month in order to placate him for Umm Kamil's sprees.

— 3 —

A month after the incident in the hotel, Saqar arrived home one evening, dragging Umm Kamil along and banging her on the head. He said angrily to his wife:

"There is no question about having to get rid of this ape: we'll sell her, we'll give her to one of our relatives on the other side of the Creek, we can put some poison in her food, but whatever we do we'll get rid of her, one way or another."

Saqar's wife got the ape out of his grasp and released her in the compound of the house. Her husband said, irritably:

"She had the boldness to enter the house of God. She slipped out of her chain and scaled the wall of the mosque near my shop. While the people were performing the evening prayer, they were suddenly confronted by her and fled from their prayers in fear, some through the doors and others through the windows. When the Imam became aware of the clamour and turned to look behind him, he saw Umm Kamil coming straight at him. He climbed up the pulpit to escape from her, she climbed up after him and he jumped off the top of the high pulpit and broke his right leg. Today I have received such cursing and angry abuse from the people who were performing their prayers, and from the Imam, as to ensure my being in hell forever. Does such behaviour please you?"

His wife replied, trying to justify the actions of Umm Kamil:

"But she is just an animal, a beast, she has no ability to think; your son loves her and she amuses us. Today I've cooked meat *thuraid* with okra for you and I have grilled the prawns which you brought this morning."

With the mention of food, Saqar calmed down and said, smiling:

"When they told me about her being in the mosque I rushed over to find the people all excited and the Imam limping around outside the mosque, but total calm inside. Umm Kamil was standing in the pulpit; she had donned the gown of the Imam and was chewing the wires from the microphone."

Then Saqar and his wife reminisced about Umm Kamil's pranks and antics over the course of the year that she had been with them. They laughed and came to the conclusion that it would be better to keep Umm Kamil than to get rid of her. Saqar therefore reiterated to his wife the necessity of building a strong steel cage for her inside the house, and said that when they took her outside she had to be held on a steel chain, which would have to be specially made for her so that she would be unable to slip out of it whenever she liked.

When they went back into the family area of the house, Umm Kamil was sitting down; she had taken their son in her lap, and the Sri Lankan servant was looking at the pair of them and smiling.

— 4 —

When Umm Kamil's monthly periods began for the first time, Saqar took her to the vet, who explained the situation to him. He returned to his wife and they joked about the need to find a husband for Umm Kamil.

Two months after this incident, Umm Kamil disappeared. Saqar thought at first that she was with one of their neighbours and would return the next day, but two days passed and she did not return. They worried about her. They asked the neighbours, but they said that they had not seen her. They informed the police, who circulated the information to all the stations, but no trace of her could be found. Their son cried about losing her and developed a slight fever. They advertised the loss of their ape in one of the daily papers, with a photograph of her wearing spectacles and smoking a cigarette, which Saqar had taken six months before; they promised a reward of 5,000 dirhams to anyone who found her.

Somebody brought them a sick-looking ape of a type totally different from the chimpanzee genus, and when they showed him her picture he said, somewhat embarrassed:

"All apes look alike."

They went to one of the religious teachers in Satwa, who was recognised for his ability to locate stolen property and to find lost persons, as well as for the making of amulets for the sick and for loved ones. After taking 200 dirhams from them, he told them:

"An old woman, with no teeth, who lives between the land and the sea, has taken her."

They searched everywhere, even going to the zoo; they thought that perhaps instinct had led her there in search of a mate. The person in charge told them that they were not the only persons coming to the zoo looking for their lost pets, although, in fact, animals usually ran away from the zoo rather than went to it.

All their efforts to find Umm Kamil failed. One year after her disappearance, there was nothing left of Umm Kamil except the stories of her devilry and the anecdotes of the destruction which she had caused.

— 5 —

When Saqar went at the end of the year to the owner of the shop which he rented to pay the annual rent, he learned that the shop had been sold to Ahmad bin Abdullah; Saqar would have to negotiate the rent with him. At the mention of the new owner's name, Saqar's memory took him back to more than twenty years earlier when the two of them were engaged in smuggling gold with one of the big merchants and were continually visiting Bombay to contact the Indian smugglers. The years they spent together had been full of danger and adventure. In spite of this, they would enjoy late nights out together, get drunk and then quarrel over the singers and ladies of pleasure. After the smuggling ended, they had lost touch. Saqar had heard that his friend had become rich through government contracts, construction work and building popular housing.

He asked his address and was directed to a large building overlooking the Creek. In the head office of the company, which occupied three floors of the building, he saw Indian accountants, Pakistani engineers and Arab secretaries. He told Ahmad bin Abdullah's female secretary that he wanted to see him. His feelings and expectations were a little confused. Would his old friend know him? How would he receive him? Would he want a higher rent for the shop? The secretary went in, and shortly afterwards Ahmad Abdullah came out and embraced Saqar in his arms, hugged and kissed him and said with delight, though Saqar couldn't be sure whether this was genuine or artificial:

"The friend of Bombay! What a stupid world this is! How many years is it since the smuggling days? Twenty, thirty? Don't remind me; we have become old and hoary. By my oath, what a world!"

They went into the office and sat on two comfortable black leather chairs. They talked for a time about their memories of Bombay and the days of smuggling. The secretary brought tea and coffee. Ahmad asked his friend how he was getting on, and Saqar replied that he was not complaining, at which his friend laughed and said:

"All your life you have been satisfied with your lot. All those who were involved in the smuggling have become owners of large companies, and here you are, still with a little shop."

Saqar was surprised by his friend's comment, for he had always considered himself to be a successful businessman, although in a modest way; he had a Mercedes and a pretty villa in the Hamriya quarter, and his account in the bank stood at a little more than one million dirhams. However, as he allowed his gaze to wander around his friend's imposing office and saw the pictures on the walls showing the buildings and schemes which the company had completed, he began to realise the enormous difference between his own modest success and the tremendous success of his friend. Saqar tried to ask about the rent of the shop, and Ahmad said in a friendly fashion:

"The rent will remain as it is, and if you wish I will reduce it with great pleasure. Tonight you are going to have dinner with me; we shall be off to my house in half an hour."

Saqar tried to excuse himself from accepting his friend's invitation, pleading, as a reason, that he had to lock up his shop and take his Indian clerk home, and also that he had not told his wife that he would be dining out. Ahmad would not accept any of the excuses that his friend produced and said:

"We shall send an employee to lock up the shop and take your clerk home, and there are four telephones there; use any one of them to call your wife and tell her that you are having dinner with us."

Half an hour later, Saqar was getting into a classic vintage car with his friend Ahmad. When Saqar showed his surprise at the shape and age of the car, Ahmad said, laughing:

"The value of this car is 300,000 dirhams. It's an old and rare model, made in America in the Forties. There are only six examples in existence in the whole world, and this is one of them."

On the way to the house Ahmad complained about his ailments:

"Life produces a lot of problems. While you may have plenty of money, you do not necessarily have good health. Don't be deceived by my fat cheeks and full figure; I suffer from all sorts of diseases. I have mild diabetes, mild gout, mild blood pressure, mild rheumatism, a mild allergy and mild problems with the stomach and colon."

He pushed his *ghutra* back as he talked, and smiled when he said:

"And do not be deceived by this black hair, for most of it is white like sugar-floss; the credit must go to the modern dyes. Would you believe it? I use the same hair dye as my wife."

They arrived at a large villa in the centre of the Rashidiya quarter.

Ahmad pressed a small instrument in his hand and the door of a garage, large enough for four cars, opened. Ahmad led his friend to a large guest wing built alongside the main villa. Saqar's feet sank into the carpet; he was dazzled by the chairs, couches, curtains and numerous works of art in the room. He sat on one of the chairs while he got his breath back. Everything glittered: the crystal chandeliers, the tables and the cupboards. Ahmad said:

"I don't like a lot of furniture, but what can I do? This is what my wife likes! It was she who piled up all these gaudy, tasteless things."

Saqar looked towards the right of the room and saw a dummy wearing a complete set of armour such as the knights of Europe wore in the Middle Ages, covering themselves from head to foot. Ahmad pressed a button and in came an Indian servant wearing a uniform, just like the servants and waiters at the hotels. He had a hat on his head and brass buttons on his shirt. Saqar looked at the servant's outfit in total disbelief. Ahmad said with a laugh:

"That is my wife's idea, too; when we moved into this house she insisted that the servants should have uniforms like the servants in the hotels and restaurants. Her father was a fisherman and my father was a seaman and here she is trying to make aristocrats out of us."

Saqar looked towards the left side of the room and his eyes rooted on an amazing sight. Impossible! Umm Kamil was standing there behind a chair. His mouth dropped open in sheer amazement. Ahmad turned to see what it was that Saqar was looking at with such astonishment. When he understood what had attracted his friend's attention, he laughed and said:

"That is Subahu. Some of the labourers spotted her one day in a building we were constructing and brought her to me. My wife was delighted with her, the children too, and she appointed a servant to look after her. She was highly intelligent and amusing, but she was terribly lazy, so much so that by the end of the year she spent with us it had got to the point where she never even moved out of her place. She then refused to eat. We brought a vet to see her, but he was unable to cure her and the house became just like a great big funeral wake. When she died, my wife insisted that we should preserve the fond memory of our dear ape, so I sent her with one of my Indian engineers to Bombay, where they had her stuffed, and there she is before you now, just standing there, smiling."

THE LOVE NEST

The Argument over the Price

ell your friend to drop the price."

"Are you still determined to buy that house."

"Indeed."

"Don't be in such a hurry; you'll soon get tired of that girl and you'll get rid of her. But if you buy the house it will be a millstone around your neck and you won't be able to either sell it or rent it except with great difficulty."

"I understand the sentiments of my own heart better than you do. I simply wanted you to negotiate for a reduction in the price of the house."

"You're a free man. How much did Salim want for the house?"

"Sixty rupees."

"And how much did you offer him?"

"Thirty rupees. The house only has two small rooms and the compound is small too."

"Would you agree to forty?"

"But…"

"It's a compromise solution and it's in your favour."

"All right, I agree. When can you finish the matter?"

"Tomorrow morning."

"Why can't you finish it tonight?"

"You're in a great hurry."

"That's the way I want it."

"We'll finish the job tonight and may God help you."

The Bill of Sale

In the name of the one God, and may prayers and peace be on him after whom there will be no other Prophet, I, Salim bin Khalifah, who have appended my name hereto in my own hand, declare that I have sold the house which I own and over which I have the absolute right of disposal, to Khalid bin Khalfan for the sum of forty rupees which I have received at the meeting at which the sale was agreed, and that I now have no right or claim in respect of the aforementioned house, which property now belongs to the purchaser, Khalid bin Khalfan, who may do whatsoever he wishes with the house as does any owner of property and none shall prevent or object to this. The house is situated in the Daghaiyah quarter and is bounded, to the west by the road separating it from the house of Aisha bint Ali while to the east is the house of Hamdan bin Muhammad which is contiguous to it, and to the north by the road separating it from the house of Al Haj Ahmad Mustapha while to the south is open space.

We testify before God to this, testimony before whom shall be adequate.

Recorded in Deira, on the fourth of Jamada al Awal, 1362.

Witnessed by Muhammad bin Khamis.

Witnessed by Sultan bin Juma.

The vendor: Salim bin Khalifah.

The Early Days

When Al Hala (this was not her proper name but, in the same way that her lover, Khalid, had bought her a new house, so he had chosen a new name for her, a name by which he would like to call her) moved from the house of her girlfriends to her new house, her joy knew no bounds for there were very few ladies of pleasure whose lovers had bought them their own special houses, and the majority of them were tall, beautiful, could cook many various and appetising dishes, were able to speak well and courteously and had memorised many verses of poetry, whereas the only verse of poetry that Al Hala had managed to memorise was:

Had it not been for my love of you,
I would not have come from my own land,
And would not have left people whom I knew,
For others.

She had made several serious efforts to try and memorise other verses but was unable to do so. Nor was she an amusing and attractive conversationalist. Sometimes she would begin to try to say something nice and witty but her speech would come out falteringly and odd. She therefore kept quiet most of the time, finding it sufficient to listen to what the other people were saying and to laugh at their witticisms and jokes. But she had a delightful laugh, which caused provocative dimples to appear in her rounded cheeks and exposed two rows of beautiful pearly teeth with fine lips, red like the local mulberries. It was this laugh which had touched Khalid's heart when he saw her for the first time and which subsequently drove him to buy a private house for her.

Khalid was very pleased with the house. He had been careful to ensure that it would be a pretty and pleasant abode for his sweetheart and had bought a large wooden bed from India for her and had given instructions for nice embroidered pillows to be made. He produced a large wooden box, with shiny brass studs, in which she could put her clothes and belongings, to replace her old metal box, the corners of which had been eaten away by rust. He bought her a set of china plates, glasses, cups and incense burners and he also produced a large samovar to heat water on cold winter days. He decorated the walls of the room in which she slept with several large mirrors, around the sides of which were pictures of birds, lions, elephants, rivers and springs.

Several days after Al Hala had moved into the love nest, Khalid began to spend most of his time there and did not go home to his wife's house until very late, after midnight. Sometimes he would sleep at the love nest and not go back to his family home at all.

Khalid softened completely in his love for Al Hala and her bewitching laughter. He would romp around with her, creating all kinds of fun and jokes and he would shower her with such gifts as he could afford. With her he would forget the cares of the day, the problems of the world and the anguish of the soul. He would cuddle and pamper her as if she were a lovely doll or a young child; in her company he would put aside his dignity and throw caution to the wind. They would play various games together like 'The Ring', in which he would always beat her because of his sleight of hand, and she always beat him at *Haloosah* due to the agility of her mind.

One day he brought her a small paper packet. It was a new present for her and he asked her to guess what was in it. Words fell from her pretty mouth: saffron; frankincense; oil of frankincense, gold jewellery; silver jewellery; and when her imagination failed her and she tired of guessing Khalid opened the packet and spread out a pack of playing cards. It was the first time that Al Hala had ever seen these strange cards. There was the King with his thick beard, the Queen with her smooth feminine face, the Jack with his distinctive moustache, with hearts, spades, diamonds and clubs: a new world of pleasure and delight. The excitement showed in her eyes. She wallowed with her lover Khalid in that exciting, amusing, new world. They would spend long hours playing *Al Shanis* and *Al Hukm* and other games. Al Hala's face would bloom with childish joy when she picked up the right cards and she would pretend to be sad if she didn't get the right ones and would accuse Khalid of cheating if he was on the point of beating her and would strike him gently on the cheek with her cards in her attractive, coquetish way.

A year passed with Al Hala living in the love nest. During that period Khalid felt that the days of that year were the real days of his life and that the period which he had lived previously had been a grey time, without taste or meaning and that only in this time had he met with happiness and joy.

The Last Days

During the early days of autumn Khalid noticed that Al Hala had lost her normally good appetite and that she was no longer eating as she used to do so he bought some *halba* seeds, a local tonic, and told her to drink the water from them, and then eat the seeds and to bear with its strong smell. It penetrated the very pores of Al Hala, but the *halba* failed to restore her lost appetite.

Al Hala became weary and a listlessness overtook her whole body;

she was exhausted by the least bit of activity. Despite this she would pull herself together and cook for Khalid and would force herself to play cards with him with her usual enthusiasm. But the loving eye of Khalid noted her suffering and it disturbed him. However, he still hoped that this might be one of those conditions through which women seemed to pass from time to time as a result of their physical make-up.

After a month of these symptoms Al Hala became very emaciated and began to cough continuously. The sorrow of Khalid increased and he began to boil thyme and other popular medical remedies for her. She would improve for a short time but after a few days she would suffer a relapse. Khalid explained the symptoms to one of his relatives, who was educated and who had travelled to Bombay and Bahrain. His relative told him, in an alarmed tone:

"These are the symptoms of tuberculosis."

"What is the treatment for it."

"There is no treatment."

"How is that."

"It is inevitable that the person who is afflicted with it will die."

These words were like an arrow to Khalid's heart and as he left his relative he could barely see from the force of the blow. He went through the alleys and pathways of Deira dragging his feet. He went back to the love nest. He looked at Al Hala as she was lying on the big bed. He stood gazing at her. When she turned over and saw him she wanted to get up to prepare his dinner for him. He laid her down again, gently, on to the bed. He saw that her cheeks had wasted away and the dimples had disappeared; the bloom had gone from her lips and her clear, wanton eyes had clouded over. It was as if he were seeing her for the first time and her radiant face had been disfigured by the savage hands of the sickness. He held her right hand between the palms of his hands and bent over it to kiss it as his tears began to fall and he began to moan, crying, with the sound suppressed as he pressed her hand to his breast. When Al Hala saw her beloved crying, she too began to cry which served to increase his own grief as his low moan turned into a wail and he cried, unrestrainedly, the likes of which had not happened since his mother died. He was unable to stay in the house. He felt as if he was going to die from his grief. He went out into the alleys of Deira. He walked, lost in the pathways.

He came out at the Creek. The sight of the full, round moon was reflected on its surface. He sat on the rocks at the edge of the Creek. He could smell excrement, mixed with the smell of seaweed, but paid no attention.

He began to cry again. He heard a sound to his left and turned towards the source of the sound. A large cat was eating the small crabs. He thought that this was an extraordinary sight.

He washed his face with the salty water of the Creek and returned to the love nest. Al Hala had slept from the fatigue and exhaustion of her sickness.

For seven days Khalid did not leave the bedside of Al Hala, except to go for very short periods to the market or to the cafe. He completely ignored the house of his wife. His educated relative spoke to him and said:

"Leave her before she infects you and you die with her."

He looked at him, his eyes red from crying and sorrow, and angrily replied:

"Would that she did infect me and that I should die with her. What sort of a life will it be that I shall have to live without her?"

Her condition got worse and the popular remedies did not have the slightest effect. Her cough got worse and she began to bring up blood.

Khalid would wipe it away with the embroidered handkerchief he had bought for her the previous year.

On the Thursday afternoon, Al Hala said to Khalid, in a voice now hoarse because of the continual coughing:

"I want to ask you for something, my dear, but I am afraid I may make you angry."

Khalid said to her, in a voice soft and gentle:

"Me, angry with you? Is that a sensible thing to say ? Ask my darling."

She said, in an apprehensive, timid tone, in her hoarse wavering voice:

"I want... that... you should bond yourself to me... that you should marry me..."

Before Al Hala had completed what she was saying Khalid had taken her sallow right hand, kissed it, placed it upon his forehead and said:

"Tonight we shall be married; prepare yourself; I am off to bring the religious official and the witnesses."

Khalid went out from the love nest with hasty steps and went to the cafe which he normally frequented, ordered teas and lemon juice all round, and took two people whom he knew from those frequenting the cafe. Then, on the way to the house of the religious official, he passed by the date market, bought a sack of dates which he distributed among the beggars whom he passed on the way.

When Khalid arrived at the house with the religious official and the two witnesses he was astonished by what he saw for Al Hala had, by a great effort, dressed herself in her prettiest dress, perfumed herself and anointed herself with incense, put on her mask and her gown and was sitting waiting for the men to arrive. The formalities of the marriage were completed very quickly and the official and the witnesses left. Al Hala took off her mask and her gown and then went back to her bed. She was shaking with the fever. Khalid kissed her on the forehead and began to stroke her head and talk words of love to her, how he would sell the house of his other wife and send her back to her family. Then he would sell this house and take out a loan and take her for treatment in Bombay. They would go in the big ship and would pass by Muscat, Iran, Qwadar and Karachi and how they would enjoy their journey; they would see ports and people and birds. Then, after she had recovered from the sickness, they would return to Dubai and they would bring with them frankincense, incense and embroidered bedcovers. Khalid continued with his words and chatter. Al Hala was shaking at the beginning but, as Khalid continued to stroke her head, she gradually calmed down and went to sleep and that night her sleep was not disturbed by a lot of coughing. By the following morning her spirit had departed to eternity.

Registration

Khalid couldn't remain in Dubai after the death of Al Hala; he went north for work and to forget his sorrows. He lived in Kuwait for more than twenty years, during which his only daughter married, Muhammad Najeeb and Jamal Abdul Nasir appeared on the scene, the Suez canal was nationalised and the tripartite aggression on

Egypt took place and the wars of independence broke out in Algeria and the Yemen. He returned to Dubai in the middle of the Sixties. One of his friends had informed him that the government had set up a Lands Department and that it would be better for him if he went and registered his land ownership with that department. Khalid gave the matter some thought. The only property he had was his old house in Al Ras Quarter. Then he remembered about the love nest, and the memory gave his heart a sharp jolt.

He went with the officials of the Lands Department to the plots of land. They surveyed the family house first and after they had finished with it, he took them to survey the love nest. They measured the outside wall area and wrote the relevant figures in their notebooks. While he was watching them do their work, his mind leafed through memories of his time with Al Hala like the pages in a book. Over there was where she used to cook while the smoke from the burning wood would go into her dear eyes and make them water; over there was where they used to play *Haloosah*. He wanted to go into the room where they used to sleep together; half the door was broken off, he pushed the other half and went in. He saw the wreckage of the bed, covered with dust and rubbish. At the door of the bathroom was the dead body of a dog. The smell was abominable. He withdrew accompanied by thoughts of death, nonexistence and the end of man and things generally.

The Letter

Khalid worked as a messenger in one of the girls' schools. One day, one of his acquaintances came to him and said, giving him the good news:

"I have just come from the Municipality; they want to see you."

"And what do they want with me?"

"They are going to give you some compensation."

"Compensation for what?"

"For your house in the Daghaiyah quarter."

Khalid went to the Municipality and asked for the compensation section. He was guided to it, passed greetings on entering and sat down. He was apprehensive for he was not accustomed to frequenting government offices. The official was talking to one of his colleagues excitedly, about the victory of Al Ahli sports club and how they had wiped the ground with the opposition in the final league game. The official was handing round a box of sweets, which was on the table in front of him, to everyone who came into the office. He became aware of the presence of Khalid and offered him the box. Khalid took a small sweet and muttered his thanks.

The official said, with a smile:

"Yes? What can I do for you?"

Khalid said, nervously, in a low voice:

"I'm Khalid Khalfan. I have come for the compensation."

The official referred to a list which was in front of him:

"Khalid... Khalid... Khalid... yes, Khalid Khalfan... the Daghaiyah quarter... they have taken the whole house. The total compensation amounts to one million, fifty-four thousand and eight hundred dirhams... sign here... congratulations to you... you will get the cheque from the second office on the right."

THE VISIT

A ll the local and other Arab proverbs about how a daughter resembles her mother only serve to prove the opposite as far as Buthaina and her mother are concerned. In their case, the mother is a scandalmonger while the daughter is quiet and reserved. The mother is towering and fat and the daughter is short and slim. The mother is overpowering and the daughter humble, the mother domineering and forbidding while the daughter is adaptable and submissive. The mother is bold and the daughter reticent. Again, the mother is belligerent and antagonistic but the daughter is placid and amiable. In outward appearance, character and behaviour, the mother and the daughter are total opposites. Even the colour of their skin is different, the mother being white, just as if she were a farmer's wife from the Balkans, while the daughter has the same dark skin as the girls from the Punjab.

All these differences in build and colouring, together with all the disparities in behaviour and personality, make for an uneasy relationship between the mother and her daughter.

— 2 —

On Tuesday afternoon, Buthaina wanted to visit her girl friend Iman, who worked with her in the same school, and who had suddenly on Monday morning come down with severe abdominal pains and consequently been taken to hospital. The doctors had immediately diagnosed appendicitis, and insisted on an operation the same day; otherwise, her very life could have been threatened. Her father came to the hospital and signed the necessary papers at once, and, by that afternoon, Iman was lying exhausted in her room at the hospital, after a small piece of her body, which had almost taken her life, had been removed.

Buthaina had arranged the visit with her friend Khulud, who had recently bought a small American car and badly wanted to try it out by taking it for some longer drives in and around Dubai. They agreed on what kind of presents they would buy for Iman; Buthaina would buy a bunch of flowers, while Khulud would get her a box of chocolates. After they had visited Iman, the plan was that they would take advantage of that lovely autumn afternoon with an excursion which would begin with buying cassettes of new songs by the female singer Rabab and the male singer Abdul Karim Abdul Qadir, after which they would make a quick trip in the new car to Awir and Khawanij and the desert areas around Dubai and see the autumn sun, that flaming orange ball, as it sank softly between the sand dunes. Then they would stop at one of the restaurants in Al Wahda street in Sharjah and buy a light dinner, some meat pastries for Buthaina and cheese pastries for Khulud and two paper cups of sugar cane juice. They would eat it on one of the benches overlooking Khalid's lake with its illuminated fountain and finally return to Dubai just before the evening prayer.

At four o'clock, Buthaina's mother, who had awoken from her afternoon siesta, spotted her daughter as she was getting ready to go out. In her usual domineering manner she asked her:

"Where are you going?"

Buthaina replied in a timid voice:

"I'm going with Khulud to visit Iman in the hospital."

"You're not going with Khulud, you are going with me to the hospital."

These words put an end to Buthaina's plan for an enjoyable autumn evening. She was surprised by her mother's proposal to visit Iman, because she didn't like her and considered that she was from a family of very humble origins. However, as long as fate had entered into the affair in that manner, there was no alternative, and she rang up Khulud to apologise with a few brief, sad sentences.

— 3 —

On the way to the hospital Buthaina's mother abused all servants and drivers; her personal Pakistani driver was three weeks late in returning from annual leave, the dates of which she had specified to him quite clearly. She commented indignantly:

"I know that crook; when he comes back he will invent a thousand excuses: his mother will have died, his father will have been ill, one of his brothers has been struck by a car, his village has been hit with floods and a tornado and the storms have blocked all the roads to the capital. He will come up with a heap of false and conflicting excuses, one after the other, and he will presume upon the goodness of my heart. All the bad behaviour of the drivers and servants is my own fault for spoiling them and treating them with such great affection and civility. My greatest fault is my compassion. This type of man is not worthy of anything better than harsh and pitiless treatment; the harsher that you treat him, the better his conduct and manners become. It's just like making *hareesah*; it only becomes soft, fresh and delicious after a good beating."

When they arrived at the hospital, Buthaina wanted to go to the information desk, but her mother asked her if she knew the number of the room that Iman was in. Buthaina told her, but repeated that she wanted to go to the information desk to get visitors' cards. Her mother became very annoyed and pulled her by the arm, saying:

"The cards are for others, not for us."

An employee stopped her at the inner door and politely asked her for her visitor's card. Buthaina's mother stormed at him in her loud, domineering voice and pushed the door with her right hand. The employee withdrew, afraid. Buthaina's mother cut an imposing figure with her black, silk 'aba' and face mask, the edges shining with pieces of gold, her gold and diamond necklaces which covered her ample chest and the scent of frankincense and Indian perfumes mixed with those from Paris.

All this magnificent and extensive female decor presented to the employee a visitors' card which stated that this lady was, without doubt, the wife of an important and influential figure and that any attempt to stop or delay her would inevitably lead to something most unpleasant for his future. He therefore capitulated and made way for her and her daughter.

Buthaina was ashamed of her mother's behaviour; she felt like pointing out to her that they could have obtained visitors' cards from the information desk and gone into the hospital quietly and normally, without all the shouting and angry words, but she thought better of it. Her mother actually enjoyed entering in this fashion: the belligerent, angry talk, the aggressive phrases and the succession of insults were all a delicious, enjoyable titbit for her overpowering personality.

When they entered Iman's room, all the women there stood up to greet them, and, after dozens of kisses and the customary greetings from Iman, her mother, her sister, her maternal aunt and one of the neighbours, a large chair was set aside for Buthaina's mother next to Iman's bed. She began talking:

"Cards! They ask the likes of us for visitors' cards! What is going on in the country? It is all because of the foreign employees who don't know who is who. What do people come to the hospital for? To steal, to rob, to play, to pass the time of day? A hospital is a miserable place which people do not visit unless it is absolutely necessary and for a good reason. Cards! For us! They ask for cards from people like us!"

Iman's aunt agreed with Buthaina's mother, but Iman's mother tried to defend the hospital without causing a clash, praising the cleanliness of the rooms and extolling the types of food which were served to the patients. At this point Buthaina's mother interrupted her and said:

"The hospital food is good? God forgive you, the food is ruined, it's tasteless: boiled meat like shoe leather; fish, the smell of which is enough to make a person vomit; vegetables boiled until they are like pieces of plastic; cakes and sweets with the taste of cement and soil. Do you call that food? Ask for God's forgiveness. This food ought to be given to jail-birds, criminals and killers. When my sister was in this hospital last year, we used to bring her *hareesah*, broth with meat and bread, loaves of *al khameer*, honey, butter and grilled meat. A sick person must have food which is nutritious and of the best quality in order to get well. How can he recover his health while the hospitals blunt his appetite with tasteless food?"

Buthaina was terribly embarrassed. What was all this high-handed, ridiculous talk of her mother's about the hospital food? The hospital meals were planned by doctors and experts in nutrition according to the condition of the patient. All that fatty food which her mother had mentioned would be likely to complicate the condition, causing high blood pressure and diabetes and probably sending the patient directly from the hospital to the grave. Buthaina didn't have the nerve to explain this to her mother, who would consider it outright mutiny.

The Filipino nurse came in to take the temperature and blood pressure. As the nurse was putting the cuff of the blood pressure meter on Iman's arm, Buthaina's mother said:

"These nurses don't do their work properly unless they are given presents and bribes. When my sister was in hospital she used to give the nurse two or three hundred dirhams every time she came in, and two days before she left the hospital she gave every nurse a Japanese Seiko watch and a Swiss Rado watch to the sister of the ward. These days no services are given or good work done except with gifts or bribes; greed dominates mankind."

After the nurse had left, Buthaina's mother turned to Iman and said in her domineering manner:

"I want to see the stitches from the operation."

Iman was embarrassed, but she couldn't refuse the request of her friend's mother, especially as all the people present in the room were women. After everybody had seen the stitches of the wound, Buthaina's mother said:

"People have nothing good to say about the operations at this hospital. They performed an operation on one of our neighbours for a hernia, and, on the third day after the operation, when she moved a little, the stitches burst and her bowels came out of her belly. And with our Sri Lankan servant, they opened up her belly for a simple operation with a long incision which disfigured her and made it appear as if a lion or a tiger had torn at her with its destructive fangs, and then there was Fatima, poor girl, the daughter of my sister's neighbour, who was afflicted with a mild attack of colic and on whom they performed a major operation from which she never recovered. She remained in a coma for ten days and then died."

Extreme terror appeared on Iman's face when she heard these tales of the disastrous operations which had all taken place in that same hospital. She felt with her hands, fearfully, around her stomach. Buthaina was disgusted with her mother's comments. Did one tell that sort of story to a patient who had just come out of the operating theatre? She felt very sorry for her friend; she had seen her face go pale as she listened intently to the accounts of the operations which had resulted in such tragic consequences. Iman's mother continued:

"Life is in the hands of God. No one will die before his appointed day."

Iman's aunt passed a box of chocolates to Buthaina's mother, who looked with derision at such a small box and then took two chocolates out of it with the tips of her fingers. The aunt also gave her a cup of tea, apologising for the fact that there was no coffee because the pot of coffee which they had prepared had all been consumed by the earlier visitors. After drinking the tea, Buthaina's mother jumped to her feet, and, as she was preparing to leave, said to Iman, in a supercilious tone:

"When you leave hospital, eat some good food. A woman's capital is her health. Nothing compares with good health."

This sentence was the nicest thing that she had said since she had entered Iman's room. Buthaina thanked God that her mother had not said anything more brutal when taking her leave than those few arrogant words.

— 4 —

After the two of them had got into the car and gone out of the hospital gate, Buthaina's mother said with irritation and displeasure:

"Those people have no background. We put ourselves out and go and visit them, and what is the result? No fruit, no nice deluxe sweetmeats. As for the story about the coffee which had been drunk by the other guests, I swear I'll cut off my hand if they ever brought a pot of coffee to the hospital. And then her mother, that woman with her vicious tongue and her distasteful and offensive comments; may God protect us from the likes of them. Next time, don't ask me to go with you to visit them."

A HAPPY WOMAN

ello, yes! and after you got back from the market..."

"Why are you changing the subject?"

She replied in a whisper:

"Because Ahmad has arrived."

As he was taking off his *'iqaal* and *ghutra* and throwing them on the small table in the reception room, her husband, Ahmad, asked her:

"Who are you talking to?"

She replied, smiling:

"My girl friend, Shamsa."

He smiled and said:

"Say hello to her from me and tell her that I say she should eat less rice."

She laughed and said:

"Hello, Shamsa, Ahmad sends his greetings and says that you should eat less rice."

"May God fail to protect him from evil, the dog, the scoundrel. As for me, praise be to God, my body is that of an athlete and perfect. Don't you have a mirror he can look in to see his own body and his belly which is like that of a woman nine months pregnant?"

She laughed loudly and said:

"Shame on you."

"Shame on you yourself; for two months I've been deprived of the sight of you, you tyrant. I'm tortured and suffering while you're happy and carefree."

She said in a whisper:

"My life is yours, my darling."

She then continued in a normal tone of voice:

"My dear Shamsa, you know my circumstances!"

"What circumstances, what poppycock, what nonsense, circumstances which you have used only as an excuse recently. Previously our meetings were arranged quite easily and simply; no, no, you have changed."

Her husband went to the kitchen; with her eye on the door of the reception room she said, reprovingly:

"What are all these harsh accusations for, my darling? Don't let your dear mouth say such fearful words ever again. Last night when I went to the perfume shop I bought your favourite perfume for you."

Her husband came back to the reception room and asked her:

"Where are the strawberries I bought yesterday?"

She told him:

"In the bag at the bottom of the refrigerator."

"Does that elephant ever get enough food? Day and night, even just before he goes to sleep, he wants to fill up that store of his."

"Let's forget him. When I passed by your house, coming back from the market, I saw your dear car standing outside and my heart began to pound."

"Now you are being coy with me."

"Me, be coy with you?"

"Yes, you flirt with me and then you're mean to me over our meeting each other."

"What are you saying, my dearest? On the evenings when I meet you, my heart lights up and I live on the happy and sweet memories of those meetings during the days and nights which follow."

"Perhaps it was like that in the past, but now I think the situation has changed."

"Don't be hurtful."

Ahmad returned; he had put the strawberries on a small plate, smothered them with sugar and cream, and had begun to eat them with a spoon. He said to his wife:

"Tell Shamsa not to wear shoes which are too high-heeled."

She smiled and said, cheerfully:

"Hello, Shamsa, Ahmad says that you are not to wear shoes which have too high a heel."

"That arrogant pygmy is making fun of people. His head doesn't reach up to my shoulder; tell him that I have accepted misfortune but that misfortune has not yet accepted me."

She laughed and said to her husband:

"She says that the cow cannot see its tail."

Ahmad roared with laughter and said:

"A man does not have the faults of a woman."

His wife said:

"He says to you..."

"I heard, I heard; whoever said that he had one fault or two or even three? Indeed, he is a whole collection of faults and shortcomings; that ugly pig, he isn't worth the soil that your beloved feet stand on."

She laughed, happily, and whispered into the telephone:

"I give myself in ransom for your two precious eyes, my darling."

Then she continued in a normal tone of voice:

"Shamsa, Shamsa, Ahmad thinks a great deal of you."

Her husband said, as he devoured the strawberries and sugared cream:

"Naturally I value her, I value her a great deal more than that Jasim does; he promised to marry her and has been putting her off now for more than four years."

"What! What did he say?"

She said quickly:

"Nothing, nothing."

"On the head of your mother, tell me what that scoundrel said."

She laughed and said:

"Nothing, he was just asking about your health; by the way, what was the result of that medical you had last week ?"

He said in a complaining tone:

"Upon my life, your sweetheart is ill."

She said, highly concerned:

"Nothing wrong, I hope, my dear; what did the doctor say?"

"He said it's likely that I have a stomach ulcer."

"Let us hope that these evil things are far away from you, my dear, and by God's will they will afflict your enemies: are you certain of this diagnosis?"

"I don't know. The doctor said that there was a strong possibility of there being a stomach ulcer."

After her husband had finished the dish of strawberries, he

switched on the television in the reception room and began to follow the Indian film which was in progress. He said to her:

"What did the doctors say?"

She told him, showing some concern:

"There is a possibility that she may have a stomach ulcer."

Her husband said:

"There is no treatment for an ulcer except having an operation or avoiding all food containing spices and acidic things and eating six small meals a day and drinking plenty of milk."

She said, seriously:

"Ahmad says..."

"I heard, I heard, and when was that idiot of an imbecile an expert in medicine and the treatment of illnesses?"

She laughed and then said:

"But my dear, perhaps the diagnosis of the doctor was incorrect, especially if he wasn't sure and said to you that it was simply a possibility."

"I believe that he is right. Your abandoning of me has caused me to have an ulcer in the stomach, and all the sicknesses and illnesses will come upon me now, one after the other. You will kill me, your staying away from me will kill me: you are criminal, criminal."

She turned to look at her husband, who was engrossed in the spectacle of a battle between the police and a gang of criminals, and she then whispered into the handset of the telephone:

"You are my life, my existence, my fortune. Would that, by the will of God, the illness could afflict me and not you. I am nothing without you, without your love."

"What you say is not from your heart; these are empty words, formed in your mouth only, for your feelings have changed. Where is the overpowering desire? Where are the sweet smiles? Where is the passionate talk? It has all gone, disappeared, evaporated."

She said in a normal tone:

"Shamsa, my dear, you know my circumstances, it is not easy for me to visit you."

Her husband had got up for a glass of water and, after hearing her last sentence, said:

"Why don't you visit Shamsa? She is the closest to your heart of all your girlfriends."

She complained, but with a certain amount of coyness, as she held on to the handset:

"You're the reason why I don't visit Shamsa."

Her husband asked:

"I'm the cause? Why?"

She said, clipping her words:

"Yes, you're the cause, all my new dresses are with the tailor and you don't give me any money to pay him. How do you expect me to visit people while I am wearing old, tattered clothing? Do you want people to say that I am the wife of a poor beggar?"

After he had drunk the water, her husband said:

"All right, all right, remind me tomorrow morning to give you some money for your clothes."

She said, happily:

"Thank you, my darling, and I also need, oh love of my life, some money for the last installment on the car."

He replied, returning to the television:

"All right, I agree."

She went back to speak into the telephone:

"My dear Shamsa, the problem has been resolved and I shall see you soon."

"When?"

"The day after tomorrow."

"What time?"

"After sunset; I'll go to the market with you."

Her husband then said, protesting:

"No, choose another time, the day after tomorrow we are going to visit my aunt; had you forgotten?"

She said, apologising:

"I'm sorry, my dear, that's the day we're going to visit Ahmad's aunt, but we'll meet the following day at the same time."

He kissed her, over the telephone, and said:

"I'll be waiting, and I'll be dying with impatience; during all the hours of waiting I'll be demented and frantic, excited and feverish, just as on our first meeting. I'll bring you that candy-floss you like so much and watch you as you eat it, and you'll give me some of it and it will stain our lips with its sugary threads, and I'll also bring you red roses, your favourite flowers, and I'll pluck out one rose from

115

them and place it above your right ear so that you will be an attractive gypsy girl."

She whispered into the handset:

"I would be ready to die for a hint of your perfumed breath, my darling."

Her husband , turning off the television, said:

"I am going to bed."

She said:

"Good, I'll follow you up."

He said, laughing:

"Don't be too late, if you wait too long I might be overcome by sleep, and sleep is the master, as you know."

She said, laughing flirtatiously:

"Oh, you are a naughty devil!"

She returned to the telephone:

"Right, my dear Shamsa, I have to say goodbye to you now. I'll see you at the time we have arranged. I hope that tomorrow morning you will rise, happy and contented."

"And you too, my darling, are among those who deserve happiness. I'll see you in my dreams."

She put down the telephone and, after switching off the light in the reception room, followed her husband up to the bedroom.

THE MUSICAL BEAR

I was sitting in the reception hall of the hospital. My sister, who had come with me, had gone off to the surgery of one of the lady doctors. I began to flick through the pages of the newspaper, stopping at the sports page, where a long interview with a football player of the club I supported caught my eye. I didn't like that particular player, because he was arrogant and also because he played in an ostentatious, individualistic style. However, I was sometimes compelled to support him because of my loyalty toward the club. His replies to the interviewer served to confirm my negative impressions of him:

"All local players were of a mediocre standard" — goodness gracious, and what standard are you?

"I hope to play with Maradona" — ask for the forgiveness of God, you're not fit to play with Aboud Al Mahtaas!

"My greatest model is my father" — your father is a crook, a land broker who never finds a poor old woman without cheating her by buying her house and land dirt cheap. How did this inferior player ever get into the first team of our club? A very strange and inexplicable affair. I turned to the 'miscellaneous' page and began to do the crossword puzzle. One Across: heavyweight boxing champion of the world — Muhammad Ali Clay — wrong, they want twelve letters only.

The reception hall was spacious and quiet in the mornings, because there were only a few people attending for consultations and just a few visitors, although they swarmed around in large numbers in the afternoons with their flowers, presents and bags. Light music and gentle songs filtered through the speakers concealed in the roof.

In the line of chairs where I was sitting were three men, and in another line on the right was a lady, getting on in years, with a little girl who appeared to be her granddaughter, and another woman, a European. The staff at the reception desk were directing people with enquiries to the various sections of the hospital and the surgeries of doctors in quiet, calm tones.

Before I had got to Five Across I was shaken by the sound of a screaming cry. I turned towards its source: a dark, male child, about four or five years of age, came out from one of the corridors. He was wearing a red beduin-style garment; dangling down from its collar was a long *tarbush* almost reaching the ground. His screaming broke the calm atmosphere and the music. The head of the reception staff glanced authoritatively at one of the staff members to tell her to take action to resolve the unforeseen problem. The employee, tall and thin, with a head that resembled that of a hoopoe, got up and moved slowly towards the source of the incessant noise, took his right hand and said in a strange, high voice, rather like the mewing of a kitten:

"My dear, why are you so cross?"

The dark boy then screamed into her face, which frightened her so much that she quickly stepped back. By good luck she was wearing low-heeled shoes; if she had been wearing high-heeled shoes and had retreated in that fashion she would have stumbled and fallen over backwards. The reception staff all laughed, but their boss threw them an irate look and ordered the employee to go back and complete the task. The 'hoopoe' employee went back to the screaming child, transformed herself into a cat, and said:

"Dear baby, why are you screaming?"

He screamed into her face again, even more loudly than before. She withdrew once more, crying. A dark, tubby, female employee was passing by and, on seeing the failure of the 'hoopoe' employee, said, in an aggressive and scornful tone, directing her comments to the reception staff:

"One little child, no bigger than your finger, and you cannot quieten it. What are you all going to do when you get married, with five or six little devils of children hanging around you?"

The 'elephant' employee came up to the crying child, caught him sharply by the hand, and spoke threateningly to him:

"Shut up! Shut up! I shall beat you if you don't shut up."

The dark child stopped crying, but this was not the start of peace and quiet. Instead, he grabbed her right hand with his other hand and, in a flash, had sunk his strong, sharp teeth, which were like the surface of a rasp, into her plump hand. She pulled her hand away smartly from the teeth of the little savage, and screamed loudly, with short, intermittent cries, spinning around in circles at the same time.

The reception staff all burst out laughing at the 'elephant' staff member who had been bitten; even the 'hoopoe', in spite of her tears, couldn't resist a smile, then a laugh, and, finally a loud guffaw at the fate of the 'elephant', who had been threatening and scoffing only a few moments before.

Then a nurse wearing a veil arrived and sat next to the child. Cautiously stroking his head, she read the opening chapter of the Quran. He screamed more loudly. She followed this with the 'Allegiance' chapter, but he did not stop, so she then read the 'Dawn' chapter. He continued to cry, and she read the final chapter, 'The People', but his screaming only increased. The veiled nurse then resigned herself to the situation and said, in a pessimistic tone, as she was leaving:

"Where are his parents?"

A Filipino nurse saw what was happening and tried to help solve the problem. She went to the small human trumpet and said, smilingly, in her broken Arabic:

"Dearie, dearie, where father for you, where mama for you?"

The reaction of the little human trumpet to the questions of the Filipino nurse was a series of high, discordant tunes. She spoke to him in English: more irritating tunes. She spoke next in the Filipino language of Tagalog: further discordant tunes, which caused her to leave the place in record time.

The reception staff contacted the public relations section, and after a short time one of their staff arrived. He was a tall, thin youth, a male version of the 'hoopoe', with a cold, unconcerned look on his face. He stood close to the crying child and asked the reception staff, in an unhurried manner suggesting extreme exasperation and weariness:

"How long has this pest been shrieking?"

"For a quarter of an hour."

"Can't you stop him?"

"No, we can't."

"Where is his mother ? Where is his family?"

"We don't know."

He did not speak to the screaming child or touch him. He said, as he left the area, in the same unhurried, exasperated, weary manner:

"Wait for a while, he will either rupture his throat or his family will come to rid you of him."

The boy continued his screaming. The people suffering most were the reception staff and some of the waiting patients. One of the hospital workers came with a vacuum cleaner to clean the reception area as part of his daily duties. The staff thought that the noise of the cleaner would drown out the screaming of the child, but the opposite happened. The high, sharp screams of the child caused the noise to resemble monotonous music.

The head of reception ordered a full alert for her staff. She had to rely on herself and her own crew in order to deal with the calamity of the irritating noise. Public Relations had announced their failure, the nurses had not succeeded, and the staff of her section were unable to approach the child after the failure of the 'hoopoe' and the serious injury inflicted on the 'elephant' which had made her jump with pain.

The only solution was to locate the family of the little devil wearing the red outer garment. The telephone was of no use. She dispatched her staff in several directions, one to the laboratory, one to the doctors' surgeries, another to the pharmacy, yet another to the maternity section, one to the rooms of the private patients and one to the public wards; the staff were all allocated except the head herself and the 'hoopoe' who, between them, answered the queries of the visitors, whose numbers had begun to increase.

While the staff had dispersed to look for his family, the child continued to scream as though chanting, and the head of reception and the 'hoopoe' were fully occupied by the large number of people making enquiries, the little girl who was sitting with her grandmother took out of the bag she was carrying a toy in the form of a bear with a number of musical instruments. The child looked at her grandmother. The old lady was having a nap on her chair and was unconcerned about the noise of the vacuum cleaner or the screaming little devil.

The little girl got down off her chair and walked along until she was quite close to the source of all the confusion and trouble. She sat down on the marble floor of the hospital and, after she had wound up the bear with the key in its back, put it down on the floor. It began to walk around her, moving its head, striking the drum and the cymbals, blowing on the trumpet and wagging its tail. The crying child began to watch his little neighbour as she played with her bear, and the noise of his crying began gradually to lessen. The intensity of his sobbing and the accompanying psychological tension did not permit the boy to stop crying all at once. However, after a minute or two, the little devil had stopped crying and screaming, and sat with his little neighbour, joining her in her game with the musical bear; they were clearly enjoying themselves immensely.

MRS KHAWAJAH

I chose the PIA flight for my journey from London to Dubai because the other airlines were either fully booked or they didn't have a flight on the day that Abu Abdullah, the director of the department, had chosen for my return. I was reluctant to disobey an order from him or to refuse him any request because he had nurtured me from the time when I started to work in his department. At first I was employed in the wages section, then became the head of that section, and he promoted me to my present post, manager of financial and administrative affairs of the department. He used to follow my progress with interest; he advised me to take courses in English language and accounts, both in Dubai and in the English town of Brighton, and made this possible by first of all nominating me for the courses and then helping me to complete them with the necessary financial and administrative assistance.

He would always take me with him if he went off with his friends to his farm in the Dhaid area at weekends. He didn't treat me like a subordinate and, during these trips, he behaved even more modestly, for he would serve the whole group and do more work than anyone else, smiling with pleasure and repeating that anyone who didn't join in the chores during these trips was idle and a disappointment.

In the beginning I had doubts about the motives of Abu Abdullah's special, personal attention towards me, and my thoughts covered every possible angle. I thought that possibly he had no sons and that I represented, to him, the son he had never had. I was surprised to find out that he had two sons of about my age and that he loved them both dearly. Then I thought that perhaps, within his family, there was a spinster sister or a daughter who was late in getting married and he wanted me to marry her. But after asking around I found out that he had only one daughter from a previous marriage who herself was married and had been living with her husband and children in Abu Dhabi for the last ten years, and that he was the only child of his parents with no brothers and sisters.

After I had examined my many and conflicting doubts about the secret of his interest in me, it became clear that these were all a mirage. I realised that his affection and his concern for me was one of the mysteries of like souls finding a mutual fondness which cannot be explained by any clear material or selfish motive.

I entered the first-class section and gave the hostess my coat and small brief-case. My seat was in the middle of the row. Sitting in front of me were two English businessmen, chatting away in loud voices, obviously quite happy. It appeared that they had consumed a not inconsiderable amount of alcoholic drink in the airport in preparation for the fact that PIA did not serve alcoholic drinks on their aircraft. In the front right-hand corner sat a blind man, with the distinctive Sikh turban on his head while on the left was a young Pakistani lady accompanied by her two-year-old daughter. The remainder of the seats were vacant.

Shortly after I had sat down, a stout Pakistani lady arrived. She was wearing Pakistani national dress, consisting of a shirt, baggy trousers and headscarf while behind her was a tall, clean-shaven youth with long, flowing hair. He was wearing sunglasses and was mildly freckled. By coincidence the Pakistani lady sat in the seat directly on my right while the youth sat on my left. The stout Pakistani lady said, in English, as she smiled:

"I am Mrs Khawajah and this is my son Saleem."

She indicated the tall youth who smiled and nodded his head and I introduced myself to them both. When Mrs Khawajah learned that I came from Dubai, her face glowed with pleasure and she said:

"The city of Dubai is beautiful. I visited it four years ago and we sailed in those little boats on the river."

I corrected her, smiling:

"You mean on the Creek."

Mrs Khawajah continued her conversation enthusiastically:

"Yes, yes, on the Creek. They really are lovely boats, and all those wooden ships, it is an attractive scene! I was visiting my sister's daughter whose husband is the manager of one of the Pakistani banks there."

Her son interrupted:

"The manager of the foreign currency section in a small branch of one of the Pakistani banks."

His mother said, protestingly:

"But he is a manager, is that not so? Whatever; my cousin Hameed is also there and he has been with one of the commercial companies in Dubai for more than ten years; he has married and has had children while living in Dubai. In addition, there is the son of one of my lady friends who is an engineer working in one of the contracting firms. He often sends some of the latest television and video sets to his mother and is about the same age as my son Saleem."

The hostess interrupted Mrs Khawajah's conversation to announce that they were ready to take off. We busied ourselves with fastening our seat-belts and adjusting our seats, watching the hostess as she gave a practical explanation of what should be done in the event of an emergency, including the wearing of the life-jacket and the adjusting of the oxygen mask and such matters. I am always amazed by these explanations. If an incident did occur, would we have the nerve to put on the life jacket and the oxygen mask in such a calm and organised manner?

The aircraft took off at midday. After it had settled down in its flight path, Mrs Khawajah released her safety-belt which was pressing on her abdomen and said:

"I don't know what the benefit of these troublesome belts is."

A pretty dark hostess came with glasses of apple and orange juice. One of the two English passengers said to the hostess, laughing, as he looked at the glasses of juice:

"Totally dry! No whisky or beer; it's all forbidden."

The hostess just smiled when she heard his comment. The blind Indian took a half bottle of whisky from the handbag he was carrying and asked the other hostess for a glass, ice and water; she went off to get them. Mrs Khawajah glanced at me as I was having a good look at the face of the pretty hostess carrying the glasses of fruit juice. She smiled and said:

"Are you married?"

I answered her in the affirmative and told her that, as a result of the marriage, I had four children. She laughed and said:

"Married men always pay more attention to the pretty girls. Look at my son; he doesn't look at this pretty hostess with the same interest that you do."

Saleem then said, commenting on his mother's remarks in a tender tone:

"But I shall soon be getting married."

"Yes, and I hope that you will show some interest in your wife. Up to now you have never shown any interest in the girls of good families. All your interest has been directed towards common and vulgar women."

She then directed her conversation to me and said:

"You must visit us in Karachi for Saleem's wedding. Karachi is not far from Dubai. Have you ever visited Karachi before?"

I said, as I tried to dampen her enthusiasm:

"No, but... "

She cut me off and went on with her invitation:

"Then it will be an opportunity for you to see the city of Karachi. It's a little congested and some places are not very clean, but it's a beautiful city, especially at night. Bring your wife and children with you; we have a large house and the children will be able to play with my daughter's children and your wife will be able to see the women's party on the 'henna day'. She'll enjoy seeing the dancing and singing and the gaiety which fills the whole four days of the wedding."

The likes of Mrs Khawajah are a peculiar type of person. Hardly have they met you and been introduced to you before they smother you with a deluge of their affection and love, just as if the roots of your acquaintance stretch down into the depths of your souls. They talk to you and treat you as if the friendly relationship between you is long-standing and deep.

I was thinking of interrupting her to apologise and refuse the sudden invitation, but she just went on with her conversation:

"We have been putting off Saleem's wedding for more than three years for one reason or another. First of all Saleem insisted that he complete his master's degree in business administration. And there was absolutely no need for him to have this degree because he is going to manage the textile factory which his father owns. But he was insistent about this useless certificate. Then, after that, came my little illness and I had to go to London and remain there for more than two months in order that I could have a simple operation. But now, praise be to God, I am in good health, strong and active, and I shall organise everything for the wedding. I know that the bride's mother, even though she comes from a good family, is the epitome of idleness. She sleeps four times during the course of each day — because of her tiredness so she says — and she cannot be relied upon on these important occasions which require additional effort. I always tell Saleem that there are many things which a man must do for himself and that it is not possible for him to rely upon others to carry them out."

Then she suddenly asked me:

"Have you ever performed the Haj?"

I was amazed by the unusual question. I replied:

"No."

She replied, in her hearty manner:

"I have only been once on the Haj but I have performed the Umra four times. The Umra is more relaxed. There are fewer people and you are not incovenienced by the congestion and all the pushing and shoving from shoulders and bodies. After Saleem's wedding I shall go on the Umra with my husband for I made a solemn pledge to visit the grave of the Prophet after the operation. We shall stay with one of his friends in the city of Jiddah. The market of Jiddah is very large and and is full of electronic products, silk materials and French perfumes which are all very cheap in Jiddah when compared with the prices in Karachi."

The hostess brought the English and Pakistani papers and magazines. Mrs Khawajah took an English women's magazine. I said to her, by way of flattery:

"Your English is very good."

She replied, happily, for my observation had pleased her:

"I studied in a convent school, Saint Mary's. Our curriculum was based on the English syllabus. My uncles protested, especially the one who is a judge who cut me off completely, but my father was adamant and I completed my education in that school."

Mrs Khawajah then became absorbed in flicking over the pages of the illustrated magazine and I excused myself in order to go to the toilet. I noticed the small bottles of perfume there, which reminded me of one of my colleagues who loved to purloin these bottles on his first visit to the toilet of the aircraft. He used to consider this confiscation as a right acquired when he bought his ticket to travel.

When I came out from the toilet I found Saleem standing nearby, talking to one of the hostesses. He smiled and said to me:

"My mother is a very nice person, but she does talk a lot."

I said, trying to defend Mrs Khawajah:

"All women talk a lot."

The dusky hostess looked at me and feigned annoyance at my remark. I took the point immediately and said:

"But everything they say is courteous and charming."

After that remark the hostess relaxed and thanked me with a saucy look as she gave Saleem a glass of juice. I went along with Saleem to the empty seats at the rear and we sat down and talked on a variety of subjects. He opened the conversation referring his marriage:

"After my wedding I am going to emigrate to Canada."

"Why?"

"I don't like Karachi; it's a difficult city to understand, gloomy, melancholy, depressing. People there don't know the meaning of joy and happiness."

"Do you mean parties, women and drinking?"

"Not exactly. All the things that you mention are there. What I meant is something else... Karachi is a weary city, a spent force, polluted. It is afflicted with all the idleness and commotion of the historical East. You are confronted by boredom in every house and store and at every bend in the road."

"Aren't you being a bit hard on Karachi?"

"No, I'm not being hard. Even if I were to stay in Pakistan I wouldn't live in Karachi. I would move to Islamabad, the bureaucratic capital, for I love the proximity of nature and the nearby high mountains. Or I would live in Lahore, the historical city with its magnificently built mosques. Karachi is an incomprehensible city in which I feel suffocated."

I tried to change the subject:

"As your mother's operation was a simple one, why didn't she have it done in Karachi? I hear it has some excellent private hospitals."

Saleem said:

"My mother is a very optimistic lady and she loves to simplify matters. It wasn't an easy operation at all. Indeed, it was a big operation and dangerous. Despite all the advances made in medicine, open heart surgery is still one of the most delicate operations and takes several hours. However, my mother's operation was successful. The professor who carried out the operation has already confirmed to us that, if my mother follows a specific diet and style of living, she has many years of life ahead of her, perhaps as many as fifteen or twenty years."

I asked him:

"Are you her only son?"

"Yes, but I have three sisters."

Our conversation turned to memories of school and its novel incidents, the countries and the cities which we had visited and the situations and illnesses to which we had been exposed during our childhood. Then came the stories of our affairs, both the successes and the failures.

The Pakistani lady in the front row was playing with her baby girl, petting it, and it was laughing happily and cheerfully. One of the hostesses was looking at the pair of them with affection and interest, while the two Englishmen had made friends with the blind Indian who had presented them with a second half bottle of whisky which he had been keeping in his bag. I don't know if they had paid him for it or if he had made them a present of it. But after a few minutes the yellow glasses were being raised and toasts were being exchanged and the laughing was getting louder while the dusky, good-looking hostess was watching them and smiling. The sounds of fun and laughter increased.

I excused myself from Saleem and told him that I wanted to go and sleep for an hour, at least, for I was weary, having been awake for the whole of the previous night. I went to the row where I had been sitting and chose the seat next to the window on the right-hand side. Mrs Khawajah said that she too wanted to sleep for a while and she chose the seat by the window on the left hand side of the same row.

— 2 —

I took off my shoes and put on the comfortable socks the hostess had given me at the beginning of our flight. I pushed my seat-back into reclining position, pulled the blanket which the hostess had brought over myself and then gradually slipped in the realm of sleep, the peaceful whine of the aircraft making me drowsy like a child being rocked by a compassionate hand in its cradle. After a short time the dreams started to arrive in the same form as they always came to me, extraordinary, broken up, in pieces, short and superimposed.

I find it very odd when someone relates to me a long dream with a clear story and consecutive, logical events in an acceptable form. Since I was a child I cannot remember having had a single dream in this form. My dreams on the aircraft were very distorted. In the beginning I saw myself in a place selling stamps and I was examining a stamp on which was a picture of a chess-board. One of my friends, whose hobby was stamp collecting, appeared, snatched it out of my hand and raced away. I ran after him. We passed through alleys, side roads and passages which resembled the alleys of the Shindagha quarter. The friend who had stolen the stamp then disappeared, while the little road led me out on to Trafalgar Square in London. Children were feeding the birds with seeds and bits of bread next to Nelson's Column. The birds were not pigeons but owls of different colours, green, red, blue and yellow. These owls were insulting the children after eating the food which they were giving to them.

Then the scene changed from the owls and I saw a girl friend whom I used to know who had deceived me with another man. She was sitting in a large restaurant, fitted with classical wooden furniture, while I was sitting under the table at which she was seated, on all fours, like a dog tied by the neck with a dirty gold chain. She was smoking a cigarette with a very long filter. She would insult the waiters and then throw the ash of the cigarette in my face. The scene changed. I was the one sitting at the table while she was tied up with the dirty gold chain and I would throw some of the left overs to her which she would eat ravenously. Then, after I had finished my cigarette, I stubbed it out in her face. Several different scenes followed after that. I was in a wasteland, the earth of which was white, and I was treading on dead cats. In another scene I was standing on the top floor of a very high building and casting a fishing hook into a street, crowded with people and vehicles, while in a different scene I was trying on my wife's earrings and necklaces.

I awoke when the aircraft suddenly hit turbulence. It was dark everywhere; I rubbed my eyes and got up to go to the toilet. On one of the seats in the centre I saw the dark hostess; she had placed a scarf over her head and was reading from a small book. As I got closer to her I realised that she was reading from the Quran. Before I reached the toilet I met the other hostess. She informed me, in a voice overcome by emotion:

"Mrs Khawajah has died."

It was a shock like a slap in the face, a blow which drove sleep completely out of my system. I said:

"When?"

"Three quarters of an hour ago."

"How did you come to know?"

"Her son went to wake her up to give her the medicine prescribed for her, but she did not wake up. We asked for the help of a doctor who was in the tourist class. After he had examined her he confirmed that she had died."

"Where is her son?"

"In the toilet."

I went back to the seat where I had been sleeping. My gaze went towards the seat of Mrs Khawajah. She had been covered up with a yellow cover. I looked at my watch; two hours remained before our arrival in Dubai.

Six months earlier I had been in the fish market on the Dubai side of the Creek. It was eight o'clock in the morning. People were crowding around near where the freezers for the fish were on the bank of the Creek. I heard words coming from different directions — a dead man — he was very old — he fell in the Creek — perhaps he had an epileptic fit — does anyone know who he is — where is his family — have you informed the police — there is no God but God — the water of the Creek is very cold — did he fall in from the Dubai side or from one of the ships — the time of death for every person is decreed — he who dies in the sea dies the death of a martyr. I moved closer to the centre of the ring of people. I saw the eyes of the emaciated corpse; they were open. I recalled the saying of the Prophet:

People are normally asleep;
only when they die do they awaken.

The ambulance arrived and the people began to disperse, some of them following the crew of the ambulance to their vehicle, with its piercing siren which then began to announce the drowning of the man in the Creek through the streets of the city.

When I was ten, my grandmother, who was living with us, died. All that night, while her body lay in our house, my father sat by her head, reading the Quran, while my mother and my sister were crying and trying to prevent me from going to my grandmother's room. When I went to sleep that night I dreamt that my grandmother had turned into a white dove and had flown off with some men in white clothes and with white beards.

Saleem appeared. I embraced him as I offered my condolences. He began to weep, softly, on my chest. The hostess brought him a glass of cold water and some tissues. We fell silent. I said, hoping to comfort him:

"Indeed, my mother died eight years ago."

He nodded his head but made no comment. Then I wondered what would happen if Abu Abdullah died. Would I retain my appointment? I didn't think so. There could be no doubt that the new director would carry out a series of transfers which would deprive me of my position and cause me to be moved to a section of less importance. Death is a sudden termination of the passage of life, a fracture to the rhythm of human activity which cannot be reset. How obscure and abstruse it is, and yet, at the same time, how comprehensible and simple. A sentence of the philosopher Voltaire which I had read came to mind. It says:

"All things existing, all creatures and animals which live on the face of this earth, must, sooner or later, die. But the only animal which knows for sure that it is going to die is the human being."

This is true, an extraordinary fact. In one of the books of religious teaching and exhortation I had read a saying of the Prophet:

If cattle knew about death, as you do,
you would never eat from a fat one.

I looked in the direction of Mrs Khawajah, covered by the yellow blanket and then turned to Saleem, sitting on my right. He took a packet of tablets out of his pocket, took one from it and swallowed it. I asked him about it and he said:

"It's a valium tablet to sooth the nerves. I took one an hour ago but I think I need another one now. Do you want one?"

I thanked him but refused the offer. After a short while, the trembling which had seized him lessened and I moved with him to the seats at the back. We talked about pain, sickness, the fear of the death of those whom we love, the death of our enemies and the fear of dying before one's time. We also talked about the times when we had seen the dead bodies of human beings. Does death occur when the heart stops beating, or when the brain ceases to function? We talked about the attempts of humans, in the past, to discover the fabulous elixir of life which prevents death; about the freezing of bodies in America where people believe that the human race, as its scientific knowledge progresses, will ultimately be able to restore life to them; about the decorated Chinese graves in the countries of South East Asia and about the pyramids, those giant graves for worshipping the dead. He spoke about the learned man Buddha and his philosophy of death and I told him about death in the film of the Swedish producer Ingmar Bergman, *The Seventh Seal*. We talked about collective death in war, disasters, earthquakes and floods, about the loss of identity and the possibility of speaking to those in the grave.

During the course of this conversation on the subject of death, we were attempting to come to terms with our distress, our fears and agitation. We were trying to overcome our fright and depression and, to a degree, we succeeded. At least we broke the tyranny of silence. Saleem's tears disappeared and, although his voice had the sound of a man sedated, his eyes were clear, in spite of being slightly red. The hostess arrived to inform us that we were on the point of arriving in Dubai, that the pilot had been in touch with the airport and that an ambulance would be waiting. I looked at our companions of the trip. The blind Indian was stretched out in his seat. I couldn't tell if he was asleep or awake. The two Englishmen were quiet. One was reading a book while the other was silent and bewildered, staring at the back of the seat in front of him. The young Pakistani woman was rocking her child in her lap as she had a whispered conversation with one of the hostesses.

— 3 —

When we arrived at Dubai airport, the ambulance men placed the body of Mrs Khawajah on a stretcher. As we disembarked, the clock indicated that it was half past eleven. The weather was dry; the darkness was illuminated by the airport lights. The rear of the ambulance was open and the stretcher with Mrs Khawajah was placed inside. I embraced Saleem, kissed him, offered my condolences and said farewell. He said to me, smiling emotionally:

"This is life; promise me that you will attend my wedding in Karachi."

I said to him, fervently, as I nodded my head:

"I promise, I shall certainly attend."

"And you will bring your wife and children."

"Yes, I shall bring my wife and the children."

Saleem got into the vehicle with the nurse, to sit with his mother inside. He waved to me and closed the door of the ambulance. The vehicle moved off, with its lights flashing red and yellow but silently, without the sound of the strident siren.

ROAD ACCIDENTS

 see the mist is getting thicker. Why don't we go back to the flat?"

"Go back to the flat and spend the weekend there?"

"Why not?"

"We haven't yet got to the big roundabout where the road begins; the mist, which I suspect only covers the city of Abu Dhabi, will lift and the road to Dubai will be clear. Why are you so pessimistic? Anyway, what is your point about going back to the flat? I haven't seen my friends in Sharjah for two weeks, my sisters are longing to see me, your daughter, whom you left with your mother, is sick; go back to the flat? What kind of talk is this?"

"Don't misunderstand me. Most of the accidents on this road take place on the days when the mist is heavy and the greater part of them are extremely terrifying. We see the pictures of them in the papers, with blood all over the place. It's now ten o'clock and the darkness and the mist will combine against us. Also, some of the other drivers may be drowsy or drunk and could smash up our little car."

"God save us from such gloomy thoughts. Our car is a Porsche, strong and made of steel, and even if there is a slight mist, this calls for the other drivers to be more careful. 'If you are optimistic that all will be well, then it will be so.' You used to repeat this wise saying often. Have you forgotten about it?"

Silence… a feeling of depression embraced the mind. The sound of the car's engine was irritating. He started the windscreen wiper and pushed in the car's cigarette lighter; he was going to smoke. She found the smoke of cigarettes so irritating. Many was the time when she had wanted to tell him about this but she never did.

The speed of the car increased; 80, 90, 100. She looked at her hands. The palms of her hands were dry, her fingers were dry. She had forgotten to buy hand cream. She had used it in the past for dry skin but these days she forgot a lot of things. She had forgotten to take the length of material which she had bought from the sales to the tailor. She had forgotten to buy the weekly magazines, she had forgotten to get in touch with her friend Imaan in Al Ain to whom she normally talked twice a week. She had forgotten her appointment with the dentist. She never remembered about her decayed tooth, which needed filling, except when she was eating a sweet. Then the pain would give a jolt to her jaw and her head and she would curse sweets, which she didn't like very much anyway.

The cigarette lighter popped out. He had placed the cigarette between his front teeth, his brown lips holding the filter. He touched the tip of the cigarette with the burner of the lighter. The horrible smell spread out and filled the whole of the small car. Mist outside and mist inside. He coughed, lightly. She wanted to say something, but she kept quiet.

He hadn't changed his brand of cigarettes for the past fifteen years. One of his colleagues once said to him that nobody smokes Camel cigarettes except seamen and porters and another colleague had commented: "Have pity on your chest; these cigarettes are very strong, pure nicotine." His brother had said, with a laugh: "What is the connection of the camel, that repulsive animal, with smoking?" That remark was the start of a long discussion about the names of cigarettes world-wide and the absurdity of most of them.

He asked her:

"What did your mother say about the daughter?"

"Yesterday she took her to the doctor. Her temperature has dropped a lot."

"What's wrong with her?"

"The doctor said that, possibly, it is mild bronchitis."

"When I was twelve, I had a sharp attack of bronchitis. I became very thin until I was just like a skeleton. I was coughing continuously. My family thought that I had tuberculosis."

"You never told me about that before."

"Do I have to tell you about every sickness that I have ever had?"

"No, but that was something special."

"Sickness is something special? What kind of talk is that?"

"I didn't mean that... I was... it means... "

A sense of depression and silence, once again. The noise of the engine became even more annoying and the mist became more dense. She felt that the tobacco smoke was burning her nose. She would be afflicted by cancer of the lungs because of constantly inhaling cigarette smoke. They would remove one of her lungs. She imagined the white operating theatre. The nurses were rushing in with bottles of blood, needles and tubes of varying sizes. Doctors were approaching with their thick spectacles, and their gloved hands holding scalpels and scissors dripping blood.

He put out his cigarette in the ashtray of the car with evident nervousness. His brother always used to poke fun at him. What benefit is there from the diploma and employment? Your sideburns have gone white and yet you're still grade two. His brother would always remind him of the morbid, gloomy, actual facts of life with a mixture of malice and crudeness. This had been his way since they were small, to speak with a painful frankness. How many times had he mimicked his brother's slight lameness in front of the family, the neighbour's sons and the pupils of the elementary school in which they had studied? How many times had he laughed at the blood running from his nose from minor accidents and had called him by the nickname of 'Tap-nose'? Many times he had wished that he had been an only child with no brothers or sisters. What good were they? In all his life not one of them had made him feel the importance of the brotherly relationship which bound them. Anyway, what was this relationship which was imposed upon a man, without choice?

He announced the good news:

"We have arrived at the main roundabout. Didn't I tell you that the mist would clear? Don't you see, from now on the road will be clear."

"I don't know, I don't think the mist has cleared very much."

"The mist will clear; you'll see."

"I hope so."

She had hoped that she would be among the top students in the secondary school final examinations. What a lot of homework she had done. She followed all the guidance given in the examination guide: divide up the topics for study — a timed programme — attention given to basic subjects without neglecting the secondary points — reduce the use of stimulants (no, this was the only recommendation where she did just the opposite) — understanding rather than blind memorisation. All these recommendations she applied to the last detail. But throughout the examination, she was restless and apprehensive. She couldn't understand straightforward questions, she forgot dates, names, ideas, sentences, chapters, rules, sections of the Quran, sayings of the Prophet, poems and theories. She cried in four of the examinations, and the nights of those atrocious days were like a child's trip through the tunnel or cave of horror in a fairground: an awful darkness with scarifying skulls, terrifying screams, piercing laughter and ashen faces with bloodied teeth. She dropped her dream of a top position in the results and just prayed that the nightmare of the examinations would be over quickly even if she failed in all the subjects. She was amazed when she passed and obtained a reasonable average.

The cars in front of them began to go slower and put on their warning lights as the density of the mist increased. She said:

"Why don't you put on the warning lights?"

"No need."

"But the other drivers have put them on."

"Just because they are stupid, do I have to join them?"

"But... but... "

"But what?"

"The mist is getting much thicker; the warning lights are important."

"I can still see the road. My eyes are six over six."

She kept silent and adjusted her glasses on her nose. She felt herself to be suffocating and loosened the buttons on the collar of her blouse. She reached for a can of cola and began drinking it. She looked at her watch. It was twenty past ten.

"You complain about your teeth and the cola is mostly sugar."

She looked at him with evident disgust, sighed resentfully and carried on drinking from the can.

"I'm thinking about the care of your teeth."

"And I want to get rid of them. What do you think."

"Why do you react like that? What did I say?"

"Nothing, nothing, you didn't say anything, you didn't say anything."

"No, no, tell me, what did I say? What did I say that upset you?"

"Nothing. Who said that I was upset by what you said? All that there is, is that I want to get rid of my teeth, they are black and brown and are the shape of the fangs of a wolf or a hyena."

"What is this kind of talk, what justification is there for that sort of reaction? A simple comment, made in your own interest, produces all this scornful attack."

"I'm not being scornful of anyone. I'm talking about myself. Don't you want me to talk about myself? Have I talked about your teeth? I'm talking about my own misshapen teeth which I inherited from my family."

"Your teeth are not misshapen."

"Goodness gracious, should I consider that a compliment?"

"Calm yourself down."

"It is not only my teeth which are distorted — have you forgotten that I am also blind?"

"Oh Lord! When did I say anything about your eyes and your sight? I'm talking about the well-being of your teeth."

She put down the window of the car and threw the cola can out with considerable force onto the side of the road. There was a little rattle and that was it. The thick fog got worse and he was compelled to put on the warning lights. Should he go back ? No, they had already completed one-third of the distance. Perhaps the fog would lighten in the second third and would lift in the final third. He took some chewing gum from his pocket and began to chew it.

How she hated the chewing of gum, especially by men. It was disgusting and nauseating. It reminded her of an emaciated and revolting black cow which her aunt had owned, when it used to chew its cud, tied up near their outdoor kitchen. They slaughtered it to make the *hareesah* for the wedding party of her cousin. She saw it being butchered; she was just a little girl. The loud bellowing of the cow tore into everyone's ears and hearts. Her mother tried to feed her some of the *hareesah* at the wedding party and she fled from her as the loud bellowing reverberated in her ears, entirely blotting out the noise of the drums, the tambourines, the cymbals and the shots from the rifles and revolvers.

Their little car became enveloped in the fog. Now she couldn't see anything, behind them, in front of them, to the left or to the right.

The speed of the car gradually dropped, 100, 80, 60, 40. She remained with the apparition of the emaciated, revolting, black cow chewing its cud.

He said, slowly:

"The fog is thicker now. We're going to be a little late."

"A little!"

"And even if we're very late, what's going to happen? We'll arrive tonight in Sharjah; we're not going to spend the night on the road."

He put on a tape of a popular singer, singing Nabati poems. His sharp voice boomed out, with the loud beat of the drum and the monotonous tune of the *oud*. She said, with irritation:

"Oh God, that's all we need!"

"You know I don't like this singer, or the style of his singing, but what can I do? It's the only tape in the car. Yesterday you took all the tapes from the car into the flat."

"Please, stop it. I can't stand it."

He took out the tape and switched on the broadcast from the local FM. It was broadcasting classical tunes, played on the organ. This reminded her of the vampire films, a great number of which he used to bring from the video stores at the beginning of their marriage. She looked, with displeasure, at the fog outside and said:

"Nabati singing or classical music on the organ; isn't there anything else?"

He changed to medium wave and got news analysis; he changed it again, to a historical programme; he changed it… foreign trade; he changed it… Urdu; he changed it… discussion of a university thesis; he changed it… English. Her sensation of suffocation increased. She put out her hand and switched off the radio as he was changing the station. He said, angrily:

"Why did you do that?"

"Boring programmes. There's no broadcast programme specialising in songs and music to calm people's nerves after all this empty chatter and talk. It just gives you a headache."

"You're a temperamental woman."

"Is that a new discovery?"

"No, I'm describing you in a realistic manner."

"My teeth are eroded and ugly, I can barely see out of my eyes and I'm a temperamental woman as well."

"Putting all the other things to one side, yes, you are a temperamental woman, whether you admit it or not."

She fell silent, sighed a number of times, looked at the fog, turned towards him and said:

"How did you know I was temperamental?"

"That is something quite evident."

"No, it isn't evident to me. Describe it; clarify it."

"If you thought a little about your behaviour, it would become clear to you very quickly. For a week you get in touch with your mother every day, then the following week you get in touch with her once or not at all."

"There is the housework which builds up sometimes."

"No, now hang on, that is not the only example. In the course of two months you go to marriage parties every Thursday, and then two months go by without your going to a single one."

"Circumstances."

"What circumstances? Then there's your watching one video film, on average, every day. Then you break off for weeks on end."

"Boring films."

"Don't make excuses for yourself. You're temperamental, temperamental."

"And you're harsh."

"What's this? An attacking defence?"

"No, they all say that you're harsh."

"Who are 'they'?"

"Your sisters. Aliya told me that you burnt her leg with a hot poker."

"She's lying."

"The scar of the incident is still clearly there on her right leg."

"Perhaps matters have become mixed up in her mind. These things happened a long time ago. I don't remember that incident."

"Naturally, you don't remember, but the victim doesn't forget. And then there's your mother whom you used to slap in the face."

"Who passed on these lies to you?"

"All of the girls: Aliya, Fatima, even your mother, poor, simple person, would smile wistfully when she heard that and would say: 'He was just a child, he didn't know what he was doing.' You weren't a child, you were fourteen years old."

"Lies, lies, by Almighty God lies, prattling, stupid women. Me, strike my mother? May my hand be paralysed if I ever raise it to my mother."

"Please, I don't want your hand paralysed now, while we're in the middle of this accursed fog. Don't get excited. Watch the road; we can barely see a single hand's breadth. Your physical cruelty was in the past. Now, your cruelty is of a different nature."

"What do you mean by that?"

"You know what I mean."

"Do you want this trip to be just one continual quarrel?"

"What sort of an answer do you expect from your question?"

He stopped talking and stared at the fog. She became aware of a burning in her chest which then rose up to her throat and felt like a hot lump. Her face was aflame and her forehead was moist with perspiration. The windscreen wiper went on, monotonously. Two cars overtook theirs. He shouted:

"Curse them. I'm driving slowly and yet my nerves are still on edge, while they go past me in this fog. They're rushing off to death, the madmen!"

She lowered the car window for a second time. She needed to breathe; enormous, steel hands were pressing on her chest and throat. Where was death? Let him come in his black cloak; she would take refuge in his embrace and happily go off with him into eternity. She said, referring to what he had said:

"They're free."

"A car in their way, or a runaway camel, will soon put an end to that freedom."

"The allotted time is in the hands of God."

He sighed, audibly, and clenched his teeth. A fierce headache was paralysing the right side of his head and all the devils and spirits of anger and exasperation were dancing in his brain. His hands trembled and perspired copiously as they gripped the small steering wheel of the car tightly. He said:

"You like speed."

She gave him a sideways glance and made no comment. He continued:

"Talk, say something; you like speed and fast cars, is that not so?"

"What do you mean?"

"You love fast drivers. I know everything, everything."

"What do you know?"

"That you used to be fond of Saeed, your cousin, the rally driver."

"What... what..."

"Your sister told me that you were hoping that he would marry you."

"You're a fool... a fool..."

"I'll bet you follow the news about him on the television, and in the papers and magazines."

"My God, I never realised that you were so despicable and low, you're the pits, utterly degenerate."

She burst into tears and her wailing became louder. Her crying reduced him to silence. He drove faster as if he were trying to run away from her. There was a strained silence, broken only by her regular sobbing and the monotonous sound of the windscreen wiper. He was overwhelmed by different emotions He wanted to say something but he remained silent. He would be about to do something and then change his mind.

His salvation came in the form of a broken-down car belonging to a local family. He stopped at the side of the road and got out to enquire. He talked to the driver and then opened the bonnet of their car. He moved several times from the engine to the steering wheel. He succeeded in his efforts and the car moved. He stopped it and handed the car to the driver and then went back to his own car. She had stopped crying and had wiped away the *kohl* which had run down from her inflamed eyes with a tissue. He said, somewhat confused:

"That driver is an idiot. He knows how to produce a lot of children yet he doesn't know how to deal with a simple defect in his car. Driving licences should be given only to those who know how to give first aid to their engines."

He didn't expect her to speak to him. He took a handful of tissues from the box and wiped the engine dirt from his hands.

A depressing silence, filled only with apprehension and misgivings, hung over the rest of the trip. Finally, at one o'clock, they arrived at the Trade Centre roundabout. The journey had passed without any frightful road accidents. Both of them, almost simultaneously, heaved a sigh, but it was neither a sigh of pleasure nor relief.

IN TRANSIT

S o you're a teacher?"

"Yes?"

She smiled as she looked at me after checking my learner's licence, which I had got from the traffic police:

"And you are about to become a pupil."

"Yes, that's the way of the world."

She said, cheerfully:

"A lot of teachers have learnt with us. So you completed the formalities and got the learner's licence from the traffic department?"

"Yes. I filled in the application form, they examined my sight and I paid twenty dirhams."

"Good. What are your address and your telephone numbers at home and at school?"

I gave her my home address and the telephone numbers. She went on, in a practical and cynical tone:

"The monthly fee is 800 dirhams. Between you and me the figure is high. There are schools which are cheaper than ours, but the owner of the school is a greedy robber. If you agree, we can begin tomorrow."

One of my colleagues had learnt to drive very quickly in this school. I said:

"I agree."

"Good. I'll come to you at your house every day except Friday, at ten minutes to four, and the period of the lesson will be one hour, from four o'clock until five o'clock. If anything unforeseen happens, such as sudden visitors or the wedding party of one of your lady friends, or, God forbid, you get a cold or a fever or you want to go out with your husband and the children... you are married, are you not?"

"I am indeed."

"Do you have any children?"

"A girl and a boy."

"May God preserve them."

"Thanks."

"In any of those circumstances, get in touch with me at home; here is my telephone number. As for me, I shall not miss any lessons; I am free, praise be to God, I have no husband or children and only a few relatives, and we don't have a lot of contact. A postponed lesson will not be wasted; we'll have an extra one the following week. My name is Laila."

I sensed, from Laila's practical and cynical manner, just a touch of sadness and dejection. I don't know; perhaps I was wrong.

The next day she arrived at a quarter past four, and she said, laughing:

"I became dizzy trying to find the house. In the beginning I thought that it was in the first part of the quarter and I knocked on the doors of five different houses. In one of the houses they thought that I was a beggar and didn't open the door but called out to me from inside: 'God will provide – no money – no money'. A little devil of a boy, who insisted that I pay him two dirhams for his efforts, finally guided me to your house."

On the way to the practice area Laila chattered away incessantly. She talked about the new model of BMW. She mentioned that she had looked at it ten times in the showroom and that she leafed longingly through the catalogue of that model every evening before she went to sleep. Everything about it, she said, was wonderful and beautiful. The engine was unique in engineering design and the body work was an unprecedented creation of artistic beauty which no-one could ever tire of looking at. The seats were covered in magnificent leather, which tempted her to place her cheek against it, while she would give her life for the radio and the audio-cassette player. She said that it was as if one was sitting in a special auditorium for a musical concert. No matter how fast you went, the vehicle did not vibrate, unlike those tiresome Japanese cars which, if one went just a little bit too fast in them, began to shake as if they were ill with a malarial fever. I asked her why she didn't buy one, if she was infatuated with the car to such an extent. She replied, sighing with grief and regret:

"I have the desire but I don't have the money. It's a very expensive car. Even if I could save half of my monthly salary, I would need eight years to be able to get the sum together. And I'm somebody who doesn't know how to save. When I go into a shop to buy one pair of shoes I come out with three. And if bad luck should find me in an expensive perfumery, then I will not leave with fewer than four or five bottles. As for the tailors, I believe that they benefit more from me than from any of their other crazy customers. But as far as jewellery shops are concerned, I don't go into them in case I commit a theft and get hauled off to prison in handcuffs."

We arrived at the training area, a vacant plot behind the very high Trade Centre building, where there were no planned or paved roads. The vehicles of the various driving schools were dotted about. The place was gloomy and deserted. Laila said after she had brought the car to a halt there:

"The traffic department school, and some of the privately owned schools, give an unnecessary theoretical talk on the internal workings of a car and on the traffic law and other matters, before any practical training. This has the effect of distracting a woman who wants to learn how to drive and simply makes her more afraid and confused. We begin the instruction with the practical side. Please get into the driving seat."

I sat in the driving seat and Laila sat down beside me. I was struck by the same apprehension which I had suffered in other situations, such as sitting the secondary school certificate, the night of my wedding, the time before the birth of my daughter Reem and the occasion when I boarded an aeroplane for the first time. Laila said:

"The three most important things in learning to drive a car are the clutch, accelerator and brake pedals. When you are able to control these three things you can consider yourself to have learned how to drive. They are the three foundation stones on which the ability to drive depends. Now start the car."

I turned the ignition switch, the car started and began to shake gently. Laila said encouragingly:

"Excellent, now put the gear into first, with your left foot pressing on the clutch pedal and press with your right foot, lightly, on the accelerator as you gradually lift your left foot off the clutch pedal."

I did what Laila had instructed me to do, but the engine stalled. I had a sense of failure. I had failed at the first attempt. Laila said, smiling:

"One of the conditions of successful instruction is that the car should stall at least ten times to begin with."

I tried again and I failed. A third time, and another failure. I seemed unable to put pressure on my right foot at the same time as I lifted my left foot. The balance was lacking. I began to feel that I wasn't going to learn how to drive. Why had I listened to what my husband had said? He wanted me to learn how to drive in order that he could free himself from having to go with me to the supermarket, the seamstress, and on family visits, and from taking the children to school. My mother was always opposed to the idea. She considered that learning to drive was an offence against morality and that those women who had learnt how to drive were, without question, deviants. Why hadn't I listened to what my mother had had to say? My friend Amina had enticed me by talking for a long time about the pleasures of driving, concluding by saying that driving represented a wonderful freedom. Laila said patiently:

"Do not despair; the important thing is the balance between the right and left feet. Now try again."

This time I tried very cautiously. I succeeded, the car moved, I was overjoyed. Laila said:

"Didn't I tell you? After a short time we shall need the clutch again to put the gear in second. Put the right foot on the accelerator and the left foot on the clutch, then it's balance again, the engine of the car itself will tell you when you need to change; it will strain, protest and be very awkward, just like a human being."

At the end of the hour I was delighted, right to the depths of my heart, like my daughter Reem when I bought her a new toy. I knew how to drive. Laila smiled and said:

"Now don't be in too much of a hurry. We are still at the A-B-C of it all. But you are a very bright pupil."

Laila's praise made me feel happy. In the evening I related every detail of my first lesson to my husband. He said, with a smile:

"You are very lucky. You are learning under an experienced teacher with great patience. I was sixteen years of age when my big brother taught me how to drive. For the slightest mistake, I would get several cuffs around the ear, and because of that I learnt quickly."

That night I dreamt that I was driving an old classic model of a car of the Thirties or the Forties. The car was very low, almost touching the ground, and I went past lakes, mountains, gardens and fountains. I went past people that I did not know. Some of them would toss flowers at me and others would throw me glances of surprise and amazement. At the end of the dream I saw my mother crying. I got up, afraid, and went to her bedroom to reassure myself. There she was asleep, breathing deeply like a child.

During the first week we never left the training area. Laila never stopped talking. She described her love life to me in great detail. She had been in love four times. The first time was in early youth when she fell in love with the son of a neighbour; he had wanted to marry her, but his mother refused, because of the humble origins of Laila's family, which she considered unsuitable. The second time was when she was twenty years of age when she was in love with the son of some other neighbours. This time her family refused to allow the marriage because he was a heavy drinker. The third time she was infatuated with a young man from among her own relatives; he promised to marry her but then went off to work in Abu Dhabi, settled down there and married an older woman who had received a large sum in financial compensation during a municipal reorganisational project. The fourth time she was in love with a married man, and their affectionate relationship went on for three years, during which time he kept promising to marry her. However, when she realised that he was evading the issue with all his talk about his wife's weak heart, his daughter's disability and his meagre salary, she left him.

She never stopped talking. She would go on relating the details of one story, and then going off into another story even longer than the first. She had lost hope of love, but she hadn't lost hope of luck. Once she said:

"Our neighbour, Sultan's mother, has five daughters. I don't believe that one can find in Dubai, or even in the whole of the Gulf, anyone more ugly that her daughters. The eldest is like a tank. She weighs more than a ton. The second has protruding teeth, just like the fangs of a wolf. The third one is lame, the fourth has a humped back and walks like a hedgehog, while the fifth has a chest like a man and a voice like the bark of a dog. They have all married and borne children. Luck, it's just luck."

Laila won the hearts of the whole family. She would drop in after the lessons and, on most occasions, would stay until dinner time. My mother loved her deeply because she reminded her of my sister who had been drowned in the Creek when she was eight years old. Reem and Salim both loved her because she would bring them chocolate, ice-cream, sandwiches and hamburgers from Hardees. My husband thought that she was nice because of her cheerfulness and easy manner, and also because she supported the same sports club as he did; she had video tapes of all their games and could talk about these matches for hours on end.

During the second week we began driving on the outer roads: the Awir road, the Khawanij road and some roads near a few of the new residential areas on the outskirts of the city. On many occasions, when I stopped at the traffic lights, I would get confused and the engine would stall. I would forget all that I had learned and would have to begin again at the beginning: gear in neutral, then first, with the left foot on the clutch pedal and the right foot on the accelerator and the brake, balance, a gradual pressure. When going round the roundabouts I would have to go slowly and some of the drivers would stare at us and laugh and point, which would embarrass me and make the car jerk or go off at an angle. Laila would try to calm me down, saying gently:

"Don't take any notice of those idiots. You are a princess compared to them. Do you think that they had the ability to drive when their mothers gave birth to them? You, you are amazing, in your second week and driving skilfully. That lot, when they were in their second week learning to drive, they weren't moving their cars five metres."

Laila loved to let loose with her sarcastic, allegorical remarks and descriptive caricatures. I do not know if these were ways of combating her sensitivity to loneliness and disappointment, or if it was a trait that she had been born with, or if she had just developed that way. She had a comment for everything:

"Look at that man who is driving the Rolls-Royce. Is it a head that he's got or a cooking pot for *hareesah*? And the one driving the

Japanese car, are those two eyes that he has, or are they two electric bulbs out of the overhead lamps that they use to light up the sports grounds at night?"

A young driver with long hair went past us. She said:

"The hair on his head is like a sweeper's broom. In four or five years' time his bald head will look like a water melon."

She came to me one day and she said, laughingly:

"Don't look at my hair. I believed one of the television advertisements and used the 'marvellous dye' which they said would make your hair 'irresistibly enchanting and beautiful'. They told the truth, all right, because my hair now looks like the hair of witches and those highly decorative birds they bring from Africa. The problem is that this dye will not fade for a month."

She saw a girl driving a small sports car, her face ostentatiously and heavily made up. She said:

"God save us, her mouth is like the door of a garage. How on earth does she manage to close it when she goes to sleep?"

During the fourth week we returned to the practice area. Laila said that the time had come for the final touches; putting the car in the garage, parking it between two other cars, climbing a hill and coming down it by controlling it with the brakes. At first, I broke the wood of the garage, I was unable to park the car between what were supposed to be two cars and I didn't have proper control of the brakes when descending the hill. I was in despair. After all these lessons I was not going to be able to pass the test. I thought about my poor students on the days of the oral and written tests and felt sympathy for them. Learning new skills in life was a difficult business. Laila continued encouragingly:

"Don't worry about these things. These are simple matters for a woman who has carried and borne children. After two or three days you will be able to do them well."

Laila had become one of the family. On the days when she did not visit us we felt that some very dear person was missing. The first one to miss her was my mother, then Reem and Salim and finally my husband and I. Even the Filipino maid loved her, for they talked freely together and she would use greetings and odd words in the Filipino language to her and give her some of her old dresses.

When Laila told me that the time had now arrived to go into the

151

market areas, I became agitated and afraid and tried to put it off, but she just laughed and said, in her derisive fashion:

"Don't be afraid; what can possibly happen? If you run over two or three people, no problem, it just doesn't matter. The blood money is seventy thousand for each one of them, you can pay it and laugh."

At first we went into the new and well-organised market areas, and then we gradually moved into the well-populated central areas. As we went through the gold market, she pointed to a place that sold Omani sweetmeats and said:

"I'm always dying to get some of those sweetmeats, but I resist the temptation so that I don't turn into a fat old cow."

When we stopped outside a shop selling watches, she said in a voice with a ring of regret:

"Can you believe it! I used to buy gifts for Salim: watches and perfume."

"Who is Salim?"

"Love number four. Have you forgotten?"

Laila was an excellent teacher and a dear friend. When I went to take the traffic department test I completed it in a very short time and without any mistakes; thanks to Laila's advice and her care and guidance, I obtained my driving licence on my daughter Reem's birthday and we had a big family party. In addition to the birthday cake with its five candles, we had many different kinds of food and sweetmeats. Laila was the star of the party. She sang *A lovely year, oh handsome.* She clapped and did impersonations of the stars of the serial *Open Sesame*: the parrot Milsoon, the frog Kamil and fat Naaman. She made us all very, very happy. When she said goodbye to us at the end of the party I kissed her with great feeling. I had obtained a driving licence and I had found a dear and valuable friend.

After I had got my licence, Laila's visits became less frequent which caused surprise, sadness and resentment among us all. I chased her up with telephone calls, and she would apologise and make many promises of frequent visits, but in fact the only things that were frequent were the promises. At the end of the third month after I had taken my test, Laila stopped visiting us.

At the end of the school year I was coming back in my new Audi with my husband from visiting his aunt in hospital when at one of the roundabouts, my husband said:

"Look! Look! It's Laila!"

I looked over to the left. Laila was with a new student in one of the driving school cars. I sounded the horn of my car several times to attract her attention so that we could greet her, but she paid no attention to the sound. Perhaps she thought it was one of those despicable drivers who poke fun at women learning to drive. When the cars moved off she was laughing and chattering enthusiastically with her new pupil, who was frowning and scowling.

THE TRUMPET PLAYER

His face was like the face of Louis Armstrong, and he played the trumpet like him too, and he had a smile the same as his. But he differed from him in several other ways, for he was more bulky in the body, his complexion was fair and he didn't have his own band. In fact, he played in the army band.

He always came to drink tea in my office in the stores and he would complain:

"You people in the stores have an easier time of it than all the other sections of the army."

Then he would continue, with a broad smile:

"The lot of 'em here are lazy — with the exception of you, of course."

I would object:

"But you people in the band, don't you have an easy time?"

His reply was a bitter complaint about the band:

"Work in the band is pure drudgery; practice and parades every day, competitions on the firing range, sports meetings, a lot of passing out parades; and then non-military sports and social occasions — we are expected to take part in all these."

"But work in the band has got to be easier than in, say the commandos or the armoured regiments."

That got his back up and he shifted his complaint from effort and drudgery to boredom:

"That's true, but work in the band is very boring. Every day the same music, the same playing and the same occasions; a very mundane kind of work."

"The work of the band boring? How can that be when you take

part in all the big celebrations and exciting sports competitions and appear on television too? What would all the poor soldiers say, the ones who are confined to military camps in the desert for weeks on end?"

With the weakness of his claim exposed he turned to a different angle:

"Yes, but there is no future in the band; courses and promotions are rare, if not non-existent. You have a future in every section of the army if you work in it except this band. There is no advancement and no future in it."

I felt like asking him how he could expect promotion when he hadn't even got an intermediate education certificate, was hardly able to fill in a simple card giving elementary details of himself and his job, and had never made the slightest effort to learn a foreign language or a particular skill.

But I didn't confront him with these facts. What would be the point? He would become angry and he wouldn't let what had been said to alter his opinion of himself. He was one of that particular class of people who see themselves as faultless in spite of all the evidence to the contrary. Besides, he was my partner when we play cards in the *majlis* of Abu Jasim and we had agreed on a special system of signals whereby he knew what cards I had and I knew his. As a result of this we won quite often against the opposing pair and benefited with lots of refreshments and sweets.

— 2 —

In the latter months of last year, the trumpet player's complaints about his work became more numerous. He repeated the previous criticisms of the drudgery, boredom and inflexibility of his duty, but also surprised me with a new line of thought:

"The real future is in free enterprise. All those who have entered the commercial sphere of activity are now rich men. The essence of this country is commerce. Did you not see the television film in which it was said that our city is a city of merchants? Here, we eat trading, we breath trading and we live trading. Free enterprise is life; business is the future."

"But government employment in the army or in the ministries is guaranteed work, whereas commerce has its risks."

"Government employment is not guaranteed work; indeed, it is a guaranteed tomb. All your life spent in a single, suffocating routine. Throughout the month you are moving like a tortoise, waiting for the miserable salary which you spend in ten days, and the rest of the month you live deprived, sad and wretched. The risks of commerce are preferable, one thousand times over, to the shackles of government employment. In any case, the whole of life itself is a hazard. We are born, and no man can give an assurance that any one of our children will not be killed by fever or sickness. The grown man today, when he leaves his house, has no guarantee that he will return. Only the other day, my cousin, a young man full of the vitality of youth, went out in a new Japanese car and ended up after half an hour a battered corpse under a huge goods vehicle near the vegetable market. Risk in commercial life is something normal and simple when compared with the risks of life as a whole."

I was not satisfied by his enthusiastic defence of the hazards of trading; furthermore, his merciless attack on government employment was illogical insofar as his own social and educational circumstances were concerned. I said, in an attempt to dampen his enthusiasm:

"But free enterprise and commerce need capital. Toward the end of every month you have been asking Abu Jasim for a loan."

He looked at me with a victorious smile, just as if he had been waiting for me to arrive at this vital point, and said:

"After two months I shall have completed five years' service in the army. If I resign after the completion of the contractual period, I will receive a 'termination of service' gratuity, which is a respectable sum of money varying, so some of my colleagues say, between 35,000 and 45,000 dirhams. This sum of money will be the capital for the new scheme."

After hearing about the capital, the reasons behind the complaints of the trumpet player about service in the band were clear and the secret of his unexpected enthusiasm for free enterprise became apparent. I asked :

"You really do want to resign then?"

He said, trying to make himself appear serious:

"What can I do? My resignation represents the only opportunity I have of entering the world of commerce. Life has opportunities and if one does not seize them one remains, for the whole of eternity, marking time in the same spot. Taking advantage of the right opportunity is the true secret of success in human life."

I said, as the picture became clear to me:

"But the termination of service gratuity which you have mentioned does not represent sufficient capital to establish a respectable business."

"All the prominent merchants rose from modest beginnings. The wealthy Khalfan Abdullah used to sell salted fish with his father in the date market. Salim Ahmad, the merchant, used to sell loin-cloths and skull caps in a little shop in the market on the Dubai side. Abdullah Al Taweel, the business man, used to sell fish traps and wood oil for the wooden dhows from a shop made out of palm fronds."

In order to prevent him from coming out with yet more examples, I asked him about the project he had in mind to further the realisation of his expansive commercial dreams.

He answered, completely relaxed and confident:

"The businesses are numerous and the projects abundant. There are, for example, shops selling pets; birds, animals and fish. This scheme does not require a great deal of capital; just a small shop, good relationships with the people who import the birds and a lot of acquaintances who like birds and animals. I, praise be to God, have lots of friends who keep pigeons and dogs who will be permanent and guaranteed customers."

"Are you thinking of any other scheme?"

"Yes indeed; for instance, there is a shop selling tape cassettes of music and singing. Don't forget, I am a musician."

"But such a project requires a studio and recording equipment, and all this will require a considerable sum of money."

"No, no. In the beginning I shall buy the tapes from the large recording shops. Then, after things get better, I shall move towards recording and entering into contracts with prominent singers. In this I shall have no difficulty, for they are artistes, while I, too, am an artiste."

"Are you certain that this scheme will succeed?"

"Absolutely certain. I am a person whose whole life is music. In any case, there are other schemes."

"What schemes?"

"A project for a popular restaurant for local food delicacies. An old house, five cooking pots and an Indian worker and a notice on the wall of the house stating 'Restaurant of the Nights'. The customers themselves will bring the meat, the rice and the grain, the Indian will do the work and I shall sit back and watch, and make the profit."

I was amazed at his optimism and said:

"But things are not just as simple as that."

He said, and he was laughing as he did so:

"Indeed, they are even simpler than that. You people, the bureaucrats, you are the ones who complicate matters, who are afraid of everything and who exaggerate useless considerations."

"But everything needs planning and organisation. Have you considered the detailed costs of these schemes ? Rent, wages, cost of materials, and the banking facilities which you require?"

"No, I haven't considered these matters, but everything will be perfectly all right."

"How?"

"Through intelligence and luck."

"I do not understand."

"I have plenty of both of them."

— 3 —

The trumpet player resigned from the army band and received the sum of 40,000 dirhams as the termination of service gratuity. He was absent from the evening parties of Abu Jasim's *majlis* and I assumed that he was busy setting up one of the big commercial projects which he had talked to me about. I hope for success and progress for him despite the many doubts which I had about his commercial ability. But, who knows; these days anything can happen. There are people who, just a few years ago, were taxi drivers and who today are wealthy and famous and for whom a path is cleared in any social gathering. This country, as Abu Jasim often says, is like a lottery. Our lady neighbour, Aashooh, after the increase in the number of luxurious cars which stood parked at her door, now owns taxis and a superb boutique in one of the shopping centres. Everything is possible. What is important is, as the trumpet player said, intelligence and luck.

After three months, news about the trumpet player began to filter out. His absence was not due to business affairs. He had spent more than two months living enjoyably in Pattaya. He would spend his evenings, every night, going around all the night clubs in the resort and his days on the beach with two plump girls, the first one of whom he had named 'The Tank' and the second one 'The Aircraft.' At the end of his visit to Thailand, he had spent all his termination of service gratuity and had to borrow money from a relative who happened to be there for the price of an air-ticket.

— 4 —

I was bent over the many papers which people had brought me for checking when I heard a familiar voice greeting me. I lifted my head and found the trumpet player, with his broad frame and his customary smile. We shook hands. Since his absence from Abu Jasim's *majlis*, I had lost a lot at cards. My new partner was stupid and also a chatterbox. For this reason I had hesitated to let him know the secrets of the system I used to follow with the trumpet player in case the matter became known to the other members of the group. The trumpet player talked about Pattaya with longing and pleasure. He said:

"The best place in the world, believe me; complete relaxation, no such thing as 'forbidden', you can do anything you like on condition that it doesn't cause inconvenience to others."

"You enjoyed your trip, then?"

"Every bit of it. The goodness of the people there is unbelievable. I just do not know whatever blinded me to this enjoyable and restful country. I was mad; every time I had leave I used to go to Bombay. Indeed, Bombay, compared to Pattaya is like comparing hell to paradise. Pattaya is a paradise on earth."

The trumpet player went on praising Pattaya: the food, the girls, the sea, the hotels, the night clubs, the bars, the water-skiing. I enjoyed listening to him as I went through the papers piled up in front of me. When I had just about finished, he whispered to me:

"Major Abdullah is your cousin, isn't he?"

"Yes."

"Is it possible for you to have a word with him about my rejoining the band?"

I was expecting something of this nature. I felt like reminding him of his disparaging remarks about government employment and his ambitious commercial schemes; but then, why should I spoil the enjoyment of his trip to Thailand and lose my excellent partner at cards? I said with a smile:

"There are some difficulties, as you well know, but I'll do my best."

BLACK AND WHITE

he came into my office, literally shaking with rage as she pushed aside the policeman, shouting with a voice like the sound of a thunderbolt:

"What's happened to law and order? Our country is in turmoil, with every criminal doing exactly as he pleases and nobody lifting a finger to stop him."

I tried to calm down her violent temper, and said:

"Where is the 'good morning', where is the 'peace be upon you'? Oh, Umm Jasim, we are neighbours, after all!"

She calmed down and I caught a little smile from behind the shiny face-mask which covered half of her face as she said:

"The problem is that troubles and the makers of troubles do not leave a person alone to get on with his life."

I pointed to the chair in front of my desk on the right and said:

"Please, Umm Jasim, relax. What would you like to drink? Tea or a cold drink?"

She sat on the chair and said:

"Would that all young men were like you, my son, with good behaviour and manners. Never once have you made your mother angry."

I felt pleased with her flattery, greatly inflated though it was, especially as my relationship with my mother was distinguished by her constant fury with me. She considered me to be a failure in my professional life, owing to my commitment to the police which precluded me from joining my father and brothers in their food business. In addition, she had doubts about my manliness, as I was over thirty years of age and had not yet married, whereas my brothers had all married when they were twenty or thereabouts and had surrounded her with grandsons and granddaughters. I said to Umm Jasim, questioningly:

"Good; now that you have calmed down and rested a little, who are these criminals who are upsetting you?"

At my question, all her tension and agitation returned:

"In this country a person cannot be sure about the safety of his wealth, his dignity or his honour. The lives of people have become public knowledge for every pervert and deviant."

She had reverted to anger, generalities and vague accusations. I said, trying to discover the nature of the complaint about which she had actually come to the station:

"Every deviant should be punished and every criminal must be controlled, but for a start we have to know who they are."

Umm Jasim, the veins of her fat neck standing out due to her excitement and wrath, said:

"It is that dog Aboud."

Now I know all the dogs in our quarter. There is Bobby, owned by my youngest brother, one of the breed of white dogs which they bring from India, and there is Jimmy, a German shepherd belonging to Rashid the pilot; then there is Warad, which is always barking near the house of Khamis, the teacher, and is just a brown local dog. There are also a few more dogs which are less well-known in the area, but I had never heard of a dog called Aboud. I said to her, somewhat surprised:

"What did it do?"

"Aboud, the dog, he of few manners and not properly brought up either."

Now the picture was clear; it was Aboud, the dog and not the dog Aboud: a totally different problem. I asked, enquiringly:

"And who is this Aboud, the dog?"

She seemed surprised by my question and said:

"You know him; he is Aboud, the son of Salim the livestock swindler."

I said with a laugh:

"Do you mean Abdullah, the son of the Haj Salim, the livestock dealer?"

She answered, her irritation obvious:

"Abdullah is a name given to men. This one is still a child, playing around, therefore his name should be Aboud. And the pilgrimage of his father! It is meaningless because it hasn't stopped him from stealing from people and cheating them when he sells them those mangy, diseased sheep and goats."

"But the father of Abdullah is a respected man in the area."

She struck her breast with her hand and said:

"These days any man who has money is regarded as being respectable, and as the money increases so does the respect. The poet ibn Dahir says:

> *And the goat, if it acquires money, is it to be consulted —*
> *It is then to be asked: 'Oh, thou possessor of horns,*
> *where is the house?'*

You are quite young, my son, you don't understand people. The respected Haj, of whom you speak, does not even know who his grandfather was. Money, my son, covers up baseness, low-class origins and misbehaviour. Money conceals all defects."

I wanted to stop her from digging up the background of the Haj Salim, so I changed the subject to his son and enquired of her:

"What did Abdullah do, then?"

She said, pouring out the venom of her anger upon him:

"Aboud, the dog, believes that the daughters of other people are the same as his own degenerate sisters."

"And what brings his sisters into the affair?"

"His sisters are fallen, degraded girls: every day, with these two eyes of mine, I see this one getting out of a car and that one getting into a car, and everything is carried on quite openly, with no modesty and no shame."

She had returned once again to insulting the family of Abdullah. I said to her in a sharp voice, as I tried to find out the basic subject of her complaint:

"Oh, Umm Jasim, let us leave Abdullah's sisters out of it for the moment and return to his own story. What did he do?"

"The crook, the despicable so-and-so, he annoys us on the telephone. You know my daughter Siham, my little darling, the light of my life, a perfect girl, well-mannered, the only girl in the whole area who has completed her university education and who has been working for a year as a respected employee, this dog wishes to tarnish her character and injure her pride. He thinks that there is no law and order in the land to protect people from dogs like him."

Now I know Abdullah, who is a very modest young man with a stutter. We chose him to play the part of a young woman in one of the school plays, which caused a great deal of amusement. He is the only son of his father. However, I also knew a lot about Siham, the daughter of Umm Jasim: her forwardness, her emotional impetuousness and her irresponsible behaviour. It seemed to me that it was much more likely that Abdullah was the victim in this case than Siham. I said to Umm Jasim, continuing my enquiries:

"And when does Abdullah telephone your house?"

"Every day, morning and night, in the early evening and at noon. He never stops or gets bored. It is as if he had nothing else to do except make telephone calls."

I wanted to ask her if her daughter was responding to his calls, or if she herself contacted him, but in the end I decided against it, for the provocative question would infuriate her. I then said to her in an official manner:

"In this kind of complaint we have two options. The first is that we place your telephone under observation and the second is that we set a trap for the troublemaker. Which would you prefer?"

"Neither."

"Why not?"

"Because both options would lead to a scandal involving my dear daughter."

"In that case, why do you not just go to Abdullah's father and discuss the matter with him?"

"You should ask for God's forgiveness. You think that I should go to that livestock swindler, that inferior person of unknown origin?"

"There is another solution; talk to the mother of Abdullah."

She laughed scornfully and said:

"Aboud's mother is insane; she has inherited this madness through her father and grandfather. She is a foolish, simple-minded woman with whom no intelligent person can come to an understanding. Even now, she still breeds sheep, goats and cows in her house, which she has reduced to a rubbish pit full of the filth and droppings of these beasts. People have developed and changed and drink milk from the

166

modern dairy farms, but she insists on the old rustic style of life."

"As you have closed all the avenues which are open to us, what do you suggest that we do to resolve this problem?"

"That you send for this filthy loafer, give him a good thrashing and intimidate him so that he desists from such childish conduct."

"We cannot do that; we need evidence and proof."

She roared angrily:

"Are you accusing me of lying and making it all up?"

"I am not accusing you of anything. You are accusing people and you have to prove these accusations. Our job has basic rules and principles and we cannot behave in a haphazard and arbitrary manner."

"This means that the country has no rule of law, that every crooked loafer can attack the dignity of people and besmirch their honour."

She carried on with her stream of complaints and accusations as I tried to convince her that the matter could be resolved by a reasonable procedure, whether through police action or by coming to an understanding with the family of the young man, but she rejected all these solutions and insisted on beating and threatening, finally leaving the station bewailing the lack of law and order and the domination of society by criminals and no-goods who none could curb.

— 2 —

A month after Umm Jasim's visit to the station, my mother told me, while we were having our dinner in front of the television, that Abdullah, the son of the Haj Salim, had become engaged to Siham, the daughter of Umm Jasim, and that the wedding celebrations were going to take place in a month's time. My mother commented on the subject in a tone of strong resentment and displeasure:

"The dowry is 100,000 dirhams, three diamond necklaces and four watches, not counting the cost of the parties, and that is a great extravagance for that skinny girl who resembles a hollow cane and is very dark, like some of the Bengali girls. And what makes it worse is that she is older than he is and has an obvious stoop and weak eyes; she wears two pairs of glasses. People are out of their minds these days, abandoning good looks and going for the ugly faces. They neglect the white and go for the black, ignore the young girls and go for the older women."

My mother's last remark was made in reference to my sister, who had not married, and it was a clear case of maternal exaggeration. My sister was not much more fortunate than Siham, insofar as features and good looks were concerned; her colour inclined more to sallowness than fairness, while Siham had a lightish brown skin inclining to reddishness. On top of all this, my sister was only a single year younger than Siham.

— 3 —

I was going around the fruit and vegetable market when I spotted Umm Jasim. She was having an argument with one of the Indian salesmen about the price of a box of tomatoes. I greeted her and she returned my greeting with the warmth and pleasure of someone seeing a known face. I wanted to remind her of the thrashing and intimidation complaint, and said, pretending to know nothing of the engagement:

"What is the news of Aboud, the dog? Is he still annoying you with his telephone calls?"

She answered in a sharp tone:

"That is a thing of the past, and the young man's name is Abdullah; men are not referred to by the names of children and little boys."

I went on, continuing my line of enquiry:

"And his father Salim, the livestock swindler?"

She said in real dismay:

"What are you talking about? The Haj Salim is the most honourable dealer in sheep, goats and cattle in the country, and a man who is respected and of noble character. He has made the pilgrimage to the house of God and he has visited the tomb of the dear Prophet; would that I had the good fortune to be of his great stature."

I asked my third question:

"And the fallen sisters of Aboud?"

She said, shaking her head:

"My son, people say a lot of things. There are people in our area who follow the temptations and the dissention of the devil; no-one is safe from their evil and harmful talk. The daughters of the Haj Salim have been our neighbours since they were quite small and are held up as examples of modesty, diffidence and virtue. You may put my eye out if it ever saw them, at any time, in a suspicious or improper situation."

I smiled as I said:

"But people say that their mother is demented and stupid."

"The people, people, people. Do they ever let anyone go by without saying something about them? Even the prophets and saints were exposed to the talk of evil and jealous people. The mother of Abdullah is a virtuous lady, in possession of all her faculties, and one who preserves the old traditions. She is not carried away by all the perverse, crazy, modern innovations. The old traditions are pure gold. It was how our fathers and grandfathers lived."

On hearing her final sentence, I was unable to contain myself any longer and burst into roars of laughter. Umm Jasim paid absolutely no attention to me and went on arguing with the Indian salesman about the cost of a box of tomatoes.

AFFAIRS OF THE HEART

isha had been divorced twice, on each occasion being the one to ask for the divorce. And she had been justified in doing so in each instance. When she had entered the house of her first husband, who was a soldier, she had believed that she would never leave it except to be taken to the grave. But she left it to go back to her uncle's house after one year of marriage, during which she had had to put up with a great deal of harrassment. Every night, when her husband arrived home, the odour of his breath was a mixture of the smell of cigarettes, onions, garlic and whisky. Aisha could have put up with his nauseating bad breath if by way of compensation his behaviour toward her had been decent. But the repulsive smell was accompanied by kicks, blows and ill-tempered physical violence. This was foreign to Aisha's experience. Drunkenness, in her mind, was associated with cheerfulness, joking and good nature. Her uncle, in whose home she had lived, turned when drunk into an easy-going person, who would give her money and have a laugh with her, telling anecdotes and playing tricks. He enjoyed telling jokes to the women of the household, even slightly blue stories containing a great deal of risque and indiscreet language. As a result, Aisha was taken aback by the violence of her husband when he was under the effect of drink.

One night, she fell asleep stretched out on the floor in the sitting room where she had been watching the television. She was awakened by a heavy and painful kick in her side from a boot. The force of the kick made her vomit. That same night she miscarried her first pregnancy. He husband showed no regrets for what he had done and, indeed, made no apology to her.

Once, he came back to the house drunk, accompanied by a fat and ugly Filipino woman, and forced Aisha to cook a hot meal for the two of them. Aisha was very upset, but she was so afraid of her husband's violence that she went quickly to the kitchen. She immediately prepared some macaroni and minced meat. The sound of the laughter of her husband and the fat Filipina irritated her, wounding her pride and offending her deeply.

Her husband's violence was always without any justification, and she never learned how to avoid it. In the beginning she tried to hide the bruises, the blows and the scars, using powder, make-up and various styles of clothing. But after a time she no longer felt that such methods were of any use because, in addition to the physical pain caused by the violence and blows of her husband, the marks of these beatings were clear for everyone to see and caused her more actual and painful distress than did the physical pain itself. She complained to her uncle several times. In the end, despite the fact that he had to support a wife and two unmarried daughters, he could not bear to see the daughter of his brother so grievously distressed on account of her husband, and he allowed her to return to his house.

Her second husband's tongue was even more venomous and cruel than the blows and kicks of the first. He would continually abuse her by saying that he had done her a favour and conceded to marry her although she was a divorcee, despoiled, used and second-hand. Not one member of her family escaped the poisonous, biting words of his tongue. Your father's brother is a robber, your mother's brother is corrupt, one of your cousins is a petty thief while another cousin is a deviant. Even your mother herself was a dubious character. All the members of her family were, according to him, a gang of rogues, riff-raff, no-account thieves. They ought to be imprisoned and punished.

It was true that Aisha's family were no angels, but the derogatory terms used were, in fact, more applicable to the family of her second husband. His uncle had been imprisoned in an embezzlement case concerning one of the government departments. Not one of his brothers and sisters resembled any of the others. One of them had curly hair and a very dark complexion, with facial features which were more in keeping with negroid characteristics. The hair of another was soft and his complexion fair, while his facial features were Asian. The reputation of their father, who had been away for a long time, working in Kuwait, was also not above suspicion. If Aisha's husband had insulted her when he was alone with her, then the matter would have been somewhat simpler, but he took the greatest delight in parading her faults, and the scandals of her family, true or otherwise, in front of the members of his own family. He took much pleasure, in their presence, in defaming and slandering both her and her family, his face lighting up with great, unmitigated glee.

— 2 —

When Aisha became pregnant she felt a great relief. She thought that, when she had borne a child by him, this would help in reducing the sharpness of his searing tongue. And who knows: perhaps he would change completely and become a different sort of creature altogether, one whose tongue would utter nothing but pleasant, courteous, gentle and well-mannered speech. How wrong she was! After the birth he was most indignant because she had given birth to a girl and not a boy, as if it were a matter in which she had any choice. His treatment of the baby was uncouth and harsh. He seldom gave it a kiss. Whenever the baby was ill Aisha had to take a taxi to go with the child to the hospital, since her husband had repeatedly refused to take her in his car. One day, when her daughter had barely reached the age of five months, her husband looked at the baby and said, in a mixture of indifference and remorselessness:

"That girl does not resemble me at all; God only knows who its father is."

The verbal bombshell was the straw that broke the camel's back insofar as Aisha's patience was concerned. She took her daughter to her uncle's house and refused to leave it, in spite of the pleas of her uncle and his wife that she should go back to her husband.

When Aisha's uncle moved from his old house in the Satwa quarter to the sought-after new accommodation which he had obtained in the Cordova area, Aisha and her daughter were obliged to share the room at the main gate of the new house with their Indian maid. Her uncle's two daughters both loved her little baby, pampering her with toys and dolls and making her sick with sweets and food.

Two months after they had moved to the new house, Aisha noticed a young man parking a new Datsun at the house alongside theirs. Curiosity and interest prompted her to make enquiries, and she found out quite a lot about him. He was a young man called Obaid, twenty years of age, who lived with his father, who was a widower and the owner of the Coast garage. His mother had died in a road accident and he worked as a corporal in the police. He was a bachelor and a well-known basketball player in one of the top clubs. He was fond of the songs of Ali bin Rougha and Maihad Hamad.

She met him for the first time at the grocer's shop opposite their houses. He was wearing his track-suit. How nice he was. He greeted her and asked how they were getting on. He petted her baby with a smile, bought her some sweets, held her up to his chest and kissed her several times on the cheek. He did this totally spontaneously, as if he had known them for a long time. Aisha blushed; she wished that the kisses had been on her own cheeks. Aisha's heart was set on Obaid; she loved his smile and his tall, athletic build. She bought the cassettes of the songs of Ali bin Rougha and Maihad Hamad and began to listen for hours at a time to the love verses which they sang. She was so affected by some of the songs that she would cry when she heard them, saddened by their outpourings on the torment and agony of the lover.

She made friends with the grandmother of Obaid, the only woman in the house, and became practised at listening to her chatter and putting up with her oft-repeated stories and conversations. She made a number of dresses for her on the principle of 'love me, love my dog'.

She became a frequent visitor to Obaid's house. She intervened in the kitchen in order to improve the cook's preparation of meals, but when she saw that he was disinclined to learn the more complicated forms of cooking, which required much more time for preparation, she took his place and began to cook most of their main meals. As well as this, she deliberately cooked certain types of food in her uncle's house, such as *baranyush*, a sweet-rice dish, fish pie and pumpkin pie, in order to send the better part of it to Obaid's house.

Very seldom did she see Obaid's father, who used to greet her, when he did see her, with some reticence, and rarely looked her in the eye. He was shorter than his son, and heavily built with muscles like those of an ox. His fingers were strong and hard like rods of iron, while his finger nails were black from the oil and grease of the vehicles which he repaired every day.

Obaid would talk to her at great length. He talked to her about the road accidents which he had been concerned in investigating. He once laughingly told her about the English woman driver who had collided violently with a cow as it crossed the road. When the police arrived, they asked her to get out of the car, but she refused. On their insisting, she finally agreed and emerged, blushing. When Obaid got into the car he found that the driver's seat was wet.

Obaid took great pleasure in talking at length about the matches of his team —— when and where and against which team — and the number of victories. Sometimes Aisha used to see his picture in the sports pages of the daily newspapers. Once, a weekly sports magazine had his picture on the cover; inside was a detailed interview with him, together with a number of photographs. There was a picture of him playing, a picture of him standing beside his car, and another of him kissing one of his cousin's children. Aisha kept the magazine in her special box with her passport, her daughter's birth certificate and the social security documents for the assistance money paid to her by the Ministry of Social Affairs.

Aisha would become very upset about the girls who used to get in touch with Obaid on the telephone, and would often remark:

"Disreputable girls — brazen — irresponsible."

Obaid would laugh at her comments and abuse.

Aisha's infatuation with Obaid led her to forget everything else, even her little baby; she did not concern herself with it a great deal. Indeed, the baby used to sleep most nights with one or the other of her two cousins. Why should she worry about her? The love and care which she received from her uncle's wife and her daughters was enough for her. Even if she married Obaid, she would prefer her baby to remain in her uncle's house. They would like to have her, and she would be able to see her whenever she wished because they would all be neighbours. It wasn't the first time that she had thought about marriage with Obaid. And why not? It was true that she was older than he was, but only by two years. Her uncle had married his present wife, who was six years older than him. They lived together happily and with mutual respect. During the last three months she had gone to three weddings, and at each one she had estimated herself, in her very modest clothing and light make-up, to be much prettier than the brides with their shining silk gowns and heavily made-up faces. Would any one of those adolescent girls with her telephone calls be able to care for him and give him the affection and love that Aisha held for him? Impossible — inconceivable. If he married her, then she would place herself at his beck and call every moment. Indeed, she would know what it was that he wanted from her before he even opened his mouth. It would be sufficient for him to ask her with his two compassionate eyes, and she would quickly produce whatever was requested. The month of Ramadan began. On the Sacred Night, Aisha prayed reverently. She worshipped while her heart pleaded, persistently and beseechingly.

— 3 —

After Obaid returned from the 'Eid Al Fitr holiday, which he had spent with relatives in Ras Al Khaimah, Aisha went to call on his family, taking with her some pumpkin pie which she had prepared specially for Obaid because she knew that he liked it very much.

After a short conversation, the grandmother went off to the kitchen. Obaid said, somewhat shyly, that he wanted to talk to her about something special. Her heart throbbed with joy. She bowed her head in modesty and humility, just as if she were a girl of fourteen. Obaid made the special matter very brief: his father wanted to marry her and he, Obaid, would be pleased if she would agree to his father's proposal.

Her heart stopped beating, her mind stopped thinking. After a short pause she said, mechanically and in a low, resigned voice:

"I am ready. I accept."

IN THE MUSEUM

hen we entered the museum, Saeed ran off to grab at the old cannon balls heaped up in a small pile near the old cannon, the mouth of which had been eaten away. I called to him:

"*Sa'adi*, my love, come here. We're going into the rooms first, then we'll have a look at the things outside."

He came back quickly, grabbed my gown and said:

"Mummy, mummy, there are a lot of bombs."

"Yes, my love, they are old bombs."

"Do they explode?"

"No."

"They don't count as bombs, then."

"No, they are bombs, but they don't explode."

"Bombs which don't explode aren't bombs."

We went into the long corridor. On the left was the massive door of the museum. There was complete tranquillity. Saeed pointed to the first showcase with his small finger and asked:

"What is this?"

"An old coffee-pot."

Throughout the whole period of our marriage, Ahmad had never liked coffee or tea. For many weeks I prepared, daily, a pot of coffee and a pot of tea. I myself drank several cups from each. At the end of the day I would pour their contents down the sink. He never told me that he didn't like coffee or tea and I never asked him about it. I used to hope that he would, on some occasion, ask me for coffee or tea and he would find that what he was asking for was already prepared. But he never did. I stopped making tea and coffee every day and just used to prepare them if I knew that we were going to have visitors.

Saeed pointed to the pan used for roasting the coffee beans and the mortar and said:

"What are these things?"

"They put this on the fire and they roast the coffee beans in it and then they put the roasted coffee beans in the other one and crush them to make them into a powder."

"Why do people drink coffee?"

"To keep them awake and alert and bright."

"But you don't drink coffee."

I pointed to some of the earthenware household utensils and said:

"Sa'adi, my love, look at this *kurwa* and this *burma*."

He laughed happily because of their strange names and forms, and kept repeating:

"*Kurwa, burma* — *kurwa, burma*."

"They pour water in the *kurwa,* and in the *burma* they cook the food."

"What do they cook in it?"

"Rice and fish."

"But it's very small."

"Yes, because in the past they didn't eat very much."

"Why not?"

"They didn't have a lot of money, or a lot of food."

He pointed to a leather water bag and said:

"What's this?"

"It's a water bag made of leather. They used to put yoghurt into it and shake it to turn it into buttermilk and butter."

I knew that Ahmad loved buttermilk, and I used to ask my mother, who had three cows, to send us fresh buttermilk every day. He never touched the fresh and delicious buttermilk that my mother sent, but preferred to drink the packets of manufactured buttermilk, with an abominable taste and smell, which he used to buy from the supermarket. Anything which came from me he avoided.

Saeed turned to the showcase with the musical instruments and said happily:

"These are drums."

"Yes, drums and tambourines."

"Yes, I saw them at my auntie Shamsa's wedding."

Saeed still remembers that ridiculous wedding. The whole family was against the marriage of Shamsa: my father, my mother, my sisters. They repeated, in front of her, their objections: he is married, an alcoholic, temperamental, he has already been in prison, he has never held down a single job, he will play about with you, after which he will divorce you.

She was overcome with dismay, because she was approaching thirty, and she retorted to all the objections with an answer which we couldn't refute:

"Let us assume that he has all the faults and evils which you have mentioned. I want to have a son or a daughter by him. After that he can go to hell!"

Mother could not give her a child, father could not give her a child, her sisters could not give her a child. In the end they shut up and approved.

I heard Saeed's voice:

"Mummy, look, that's another water bag."

I laughed and said:

"No, my love, it's not a water bag, it's a musical bag and they can play some lovely tunes on it."

He found my comments strange, but he quickly turned to the big *Laiwa* drum standing in the corner of the corridor. He began to bang happily on it with his two little hands. I stopped him from drumming and whispered to him:

"Look over there."

He turned towards where I had pointed and I continued, still in a whisper:

"If that fat guard there catches us touching and playing with the property of the museum, he'll beat us."

Saeed stepped back and almost fell because he had bumped into the coffee pot which had been placed there. As I caught him, he turned and asked inquisitively:

"What are those things?"

"That's a beduin sitting area, with a coffee pot, a fire, a carpet, a rifle and a box decorated with stars."

"But the stars in the sky are white, and these stars are red."

"Yes, because they are made of copper."

It never happened, on the few occasions when we went out cruising in his car for a run-around, that Ahmad ever referred to the moon or

179

the stars at night or to the beauty of the setting of the sun. Did these fascinating scenes of nature not affect his feelings? I don't know.

I said, drawing Saeed's attention to one of the showcases:

"Sa'adi! Look, my love, at these oyster shells and pretty coloured seashells."

He didn't take much notice of them. He pointed to a massive bone and said, astonished:

"What is this?"

I put on my spectacles and read what was written on the small descriptive card inside the showcase beside the bone:

"It's a rib from a whale."

"The whale is very big, then?"

"Yes."

"Could it eat us, you and me?"

"Yes."

"And my grandmother Fatima as well?"

I smiled and said:

"Yes."

"And it could eat my grandfather Abdullah as well?"

"Yes."

"And our car?"

"Yes."

"And our house as well?"

I laughed and said:

"No, my love, it couldn't eat our house. The whale is big, but it isn't that big."

Saeed turned towards the showcase with costumes and clothing. He stared at the model of a man clothed in a white *thoub* and a *ghutra* and *aqaal* and carrying a *bisht* over his right arm, and at the woman wearing an embroidered *thoub*, with henna patterns on her hands.

On our wedding night Ahmad was carrying his *bisht* over his right arm. I disapproved of this and had expected that he would wear his *bisht* over his shoulders and drape it round himself to enhance his prestige and elegance. But he didn't, and nor did he smile throughout the party.

When I asked him the reason, he said that it was so that the women who were present at the party would respect and not underestimate him or consider him someone who could be taken lightly. An odd explanation, but one which I accepted at the time.

Saeed said, pointing at the face of the man:

"Mummy, the man doesn't have any mouth, or nose or eyes."

"No, because he's just a dummy."

"But the dummies that you bring for me have mouths, noses and eyes."

"Those are just little dummies, but the big dummies do not have mouths, noses and eyes."

He turned to look behind him and saw two dummies, white and black, dressed in the clothing of divers. He asked in amazement:

"What's that?"

"Those are clothes which divers used to wear to protect themselves from the stings of fish and the dangerous sea creatures."

He said, perplexed:

"Why did they dive in the sea?"

"To search for pearls."

I pulled him by the hand towards at the showcase in which were exhibited the pearl boxes, the pearl shells and the weighing equipment for the pearls. I showed him the clip which is put on the nose, the tools for opening the shells, the diving stones, the ropes with which the pullers retrieved the divers, the bag into which the divers put the pearl shells and pictures of the diving vessels. Saaed asked:

"Why do they look for pearls?"

"Because they are beautiful and of great value. They used to live off the trade in them."

"And are they still searching for pearls?"

"No. They gave up doing that a long time ago."

"Why?"

"Because they found something else. They found oil."

"Do they search for oil in the same way?"

I laughed and said:

"No, my love. The search for oil is something entirely different."

"Will they find something else besides oil?"

"Perhaps. I don't know."

He saw three dummies representing children, wearing decorated and embroidered clothing, and said:

"Look, Mum, these are small dummies and they have mouths, noses and eyes."

I had a look at them. It was true, but why did they put a face-mask on the face of that little child? Even in the past, little girls didn't wear face-masks at that early age. Saeed said:

"What is this little box, Mum?"

'It's a box that women use; they put their perfume in it."

Ahmad used to hate the Indian perfumes and their blends. I never dared to perfume myself with them if he was there. I used to hide the blended perfume that my mother and sister sent me and never used it except when we had lady visitors, or if I went off to a wedding party. Most of the things that I liked used to arouse his intense dislike. People I would be attracted to, he would shun. The kinds of food that I preferred, he didn't like. The music and songs I enjoyed listening to, he couldn't stand. The places that I liked to visit, he kept away from.

Saeed said, pulling on the sleeve of my frock:

"Mummy, look, guns!"

"Yes, my love, rifles and revolvers."

"Did they kill?"

"Yes, and these are spears and bows and arrows."

"Did they kill, too?"

"Yes."

"Look at these knives."

"No, they are daggers, and those are swords next to them."

"Do they also kill?"

"Yes, my love, they all kill."

He pointed to one of the swords:

"How many men did this sword kill?"

"I don't know."

"Did my grandfather kill anyone with a sword or a rifle?"

I found his question very strange. I said:

"No, my love, your grandfather wasn't a warrior, he was a merchant."

He was disappointed with my answer. He turned to one of the showcases and said, with enthusiasm:

"These are eagles like the eagles I saw in the picture book which you bought for me last year."

"No, my love, they are falcons."

He began to look at the four stuffed falcons, and asked when he saw the hooded falcon:

"Why do they cover up its face?"

"I don't know; perhaps so that it can't escape."

Saeed began to look, fascinated, at a falcon which was eating a pigeon covered in blood.

His father used to love watching the televison programmes which depicted animals during the chase and the kill. On a number of occasions, he brought video cassettes of dog fights where the dogs savaged each other with their repulsive bloodstained teeth.

When we went out into the courtyard of the museum, Saeed ran to the well in the centre. I ran behind him in alarm and caught hold of him. When we looked down into the bottom of the well, he said:

"What is in the well?"

"Water."

"And that picture?"

I smiled and said:

"It's the picture of Sa'adi and his mother."

I sat with him on the ground by the side of the well. I was fascinated by the rays of the morning autumn sun, the quiet of the place and the absence of visitors. I told him the story of the clever rabbit which deceived the lion that had been killing the poor little rabbits by leading it to the deep well and drowning it there. I had known the story by heart since elementary school days. However, it didn't interest Saeed. We went into the room opposite the office at the entrance. The air there was very cold because of the air-conditioning unit. Saeed looked inquisitively at what was in the big glass box and said:

"What is that?"

"The bones of a dead man from 3,000 years ago."

"And he has got some cooking pots."

"Yes, he's got some cooking pots."

"How did he die?"

"I don't know."

"Did he die here in the museum?"

"No, he died in Qusais."

"Near the house of my auntie Shamsa?"

I smiled and said:

"Yes, around there."

He looked at the air-conditioning and said:

"Does he need air-conditioning all the time?"

"Yes."

"His head is broken. Where are his mouth and his eyes, and his hair and his flesh?"

"They have decomposed, been destroyed, disappeared."

"How?"

"I don't know."

When my father had told me that Ahmad wanted to divorce me, I wished that I could see him as a lifeless corpse. Just like this dead man, with his head smashed in, his face disfigured and his body decomposed. I hated him intensely. My feelings did not subside until they told me that he would leave Saeed with me for me to bring up and that he would not demand him, ever.

We went back again to the courtyard of the museum. Saeed liked the four small wooden boats on the right of the entrance office and climbed up into one of them. I took him down from it and he said to me, laughing at his bit of devilry:

"Let me sit on the *abra*."

"This isn't an *abra*, it's a *shasha*."

"What is the difference between it and an *abra*?"

"The *abra* is made of wood and nails, but the *shasha* is made of palm fronds and rope."

I took him to see the tent with its shady roof constructed from palm fronds, but they didn't interest him. I took him to see himself in the mirror high up in the centre of the tent. He put out his tongue at the mirror and said:

"When am I going to be a big man?"

I kissed him on his cheeks and said:

"I'd die for you, my love, don't be in a hurry. You will be a young man, handsome and tall, you'll have a moustache and a nice beard and two broad shoulders."

He slipped away from me and went out into the courtyard of the museum. He went past the properties in the last section of the museum without paying much attention to the copper untensils or the axe heads and old trinkets. An earthenware dish caught his

184

attention. On it was a sculptured viper. Beside it was an earthenware bowl, on the inside of which was an earthenware snake. He said:

"These things are old!"

"Yes, they are 3,000 years old."

"Did they like vipers and snakes?"

"Perhaps they used to worship them."

"Why?"

"Possibly to avoid the evil from them so that they wouldn't bite them."

"Is a snake bite painful?"

"Very much; it can even kill a man."

He looked fearfully at the images of the snakes and said, his voice trembling:

"Are there snakes in our house?"

"No, my love. Snakes are to be found in jungles and deserts."

✻   ✻   ✻

In the evening Saeed, worn out from the day, went to sleep. I watched a boring Arabic film on television and went to sleep at about midnight. I awoke to Saeed's screaming. My heart nearly shot out of my breast from the severity of his screams. I leaped up in fear. There was no doubt that he was having a terrible nightmare. I carried him from his bed and covered him with kisses. I repeated the *bismallah* and the *taawidh*. I dried his tears and his crying stopped. He awoke and looked at me through two frightened eyes. I poured out some water for him from the bottle on the table near the bed. After he had drunk a little out of the glass he said, in a tremulous voice:

"Mummy, mummy, will you bring me the big drum which is in the museum?"

"For certain my love; for sure, my life!"

"And the *shasha*, will you bring me the *shasha* too?"

"Yes, my life; yes, my eyes. I shall bring you everything you would like to have."

His breast was close against mine; our two hearts beat as one, while the calm of the night blanketed out everything except the beating of our two hearts.

185

THE WINK OF
THE MONA LISA

asan was amazed by the number of women. It was the first time in his life that he had attended a party for ladies. He had been embarrassed and hesitant but his brother had insisted that he, his other brothers, and his close friends should attend his wedding night party. While he was passing through the throng of women, walking with the group following the bridegroom, all the faces of the women covered in make-up, kohl and powders, the flashing of their jewellery, gold and diamonds and the colours of their dresses covering the whole spectrum, all became jumbled up in his eyes, while the various comments of the women, together with the music and singing of the vocal group, all crowded into his ears.

"Which of them is the bridegroom ? The thin one or the fat one?"

"I don't know. Why doesn't he wear a *bisht* so that people can recognise him?"

"Some of the young men don't wear a *bisht* on the wedding night."

Clapping, trilling and singing:

> *By the sweat of his own brow, did he marry his bride,*
> *With God's help, did he marry his bride.*

"Look! look at that dwarf, I do hope he isn't the bridegroom. What a shock that would be to the bride."

"No, no he's his cousin."

More clapping, trilling and singing:

> *He's marrying a young girl,*
> *the hair of whose head*

187

would hold back wild horses,
He's getting a young girl whose eyes are as bright as Canopus.

"The bride has weak eyesight."

"But she doesn't wear glasses!"

"She wears contact lenses. These days there are all kinds of contact lenses."

"Today it is a simple matter to cover up faults and defects."

"Yes, everything in mankind is repairable. Mankind now has accessories and spare parts available, ready for use, just like cars and machinery."

A storm of trilling, clapping and singing:

Our groom, a full moon at its beginning:
may all your nights be as bright,
You have taken her and may things turn out well.
She is a nymph from the land of light.

The groom arrived at where the bride was sitting. He raised the fine white veil covering her face and kissed her on the brow. The trilling became louder. He sat down on the seat next to the bride's chair. Hasan, his brothers and his companions stood on the left of the bridegroom. It was now time for the photographs. Flashes went off. How Hasan hated the camera flashes. The mother of the bride came forward to sit between the bride and the groom and a number of photographs were taken of her with the two of them; she was followed by the sisters of the bride. Hasan listened to a derisory and indignant comment from one of the ladies sitting at the table near where he was standing:

"Look at the sisters of the bride jumping up to be photographed without any modesty. They're behaving like little girls, whereas they are mature women who, if they got married today, would become pregnant tomorrow."

The sisters of the groom appeared next, but were rather more sedate.

The children of both families, in their coloured dresses, were then brought in. The hands and faces of some of them were soiled with traces of food. All this time the bride never once dropped her smile. It was as if she had put on one of those smiling masks worn by the players in the comedies of the Greek classical theatre. Innumerable cameras and hundreds of flashes were going off. The bride seemed afraid that someone might take a photograph of her while she was frowning or scowling — or just not smiling, for the comments of her friends and the ladies of both families would be merciless if only one photograph were to be taken while she was not smiling. It would be said of her that she was sad or unhappy about her marriage, or that she was big-headed and arrogant, or that she was of a complex nature and would make her husband's life one of continuous hardship and unending misery. The bride's friends then came forward and were photographed over and over again as they kissed her and congratulated her. Some of them shook hands with the groom and congratulated him. The spiteful female voice came across from Hasan's right once again:

"Women of little manners: they smile at the groom, shake hands with him in a seductive manner, while they are almost eating him up with their eyes."

She was supported by an angry female voice nearby which said:

"Manners have been lost. The way girls are brought up now is poor and this is the result."

On the right of the bride Hasan spotted a tall girl with extraordinary features. Her hair was honey blonde and she had a very small mouth. Hasan was surprised that she could even eat with it. Her forehead was very broad. These unusual features, together with her shining black dress, the front of which was decorated with seed pearls, caught the attention of Hasan and he began to look at her steadily while she was looking in his direction. She winked at him with her left eye. Did she mean it for him? Most unlikely. After all, he didn't know her. Was it a sudden attraction, caused by the occasion? No, no; no doubt that she had closed her left eye because it had been affected by the flashing which surrounded the bride. Hasan lowered his head, reflecting on that wink.

After a few moments he raised his head again and looked at her. A second wink, and this time it was accompanied by a gentle smile which gave a special attraction to that tiny mouth. Hasan's heart beat faster. There seemed to be no doubt that she meant it for him: a second time, and this time with a smile. He moved his gaze to the bride. The lights, the flashes and the psychological strain to which she was being subjected in this little ordeal had caused her to perspire, affecting her make-up. Parts of it, on her temple and her left cheek, had begun to run.

He returned his gaze to the blonde girl. Her smiling face was still looking in his direction. She winked at him for a third time. This time his blissful, hopeful doubts were converted into certainty and great happiness. This then, was the love at first sight of which he had heard so much. He looked at all his friends standing beside him. How was he different from them? If you left out Salim, who was very short, and Abdullah, who was dark, they were all alike in both features and complexion, and they were all as elegant in their dress as he was. Why had she chosen him, specifically? Perhaps because of his composure. The others were all talking to the groom and their female relatives and were moving about and talking more than he was. As for himself, he just stood silently where he was, looking at the faces and observing what was going on.

The bride and groom stood up, came down from the seats on the bridal platform and went towards the table on which the large wedding cake had been placed. Before the blonde girl disappeared from view behind the bride, to be lost in the sea of tightly-bunched girls, she winked at him for the fourth time and said goodbye to him with that same loving smile.

Hasan didn't know how he left the ladies party or how he left the hotel and got into his car. He felt that he was swimming in some fabulous sea or floating in an ethereal atmosphere. All that night he did not sleep. He listened to dozens of songs, changing the tapes of the music every few minutes. He remembered that he had seen her face somewhere before, but where? Where? His memory did not help him. He started to walk from the bedroom to the garden, then inside the sitting room. It was after half past three in the morning. Everybody was asleep, his father, mother, brothers and sisters. He put the light on and went to the bookcase. He began to go through some books of poetry. He flicked over the pages of the anthology of Jamil Buthaina and found, delighted, a verse in which it said:

If she had left me with my senses, I would not be wanting her,
but my wanting her comes after I have lost my senses.

He put the anthology back into its place and turned to look at the lower part of the table lamp in front of the bookcase. There he saw a picture of her. His heart beat furiously, it was she! He grabbed the picture. It was a small and beautiful copy of the Mona Lisa, the masterpiece of Leonardo Da Vinci. His brother Khalid, who read a great deal, had bought it in an antique shop in the Portobello Road in London when he was there for treatment after one of the public transport buses had knocked him down and broken both his legs. Yes, it really was her, with her broad forehead, her tiny mouth and full face. He took the picture with him to his bedroom and sat there, dreaming the sweetest and most blissful of dreams until the sun rose.

— 2 —

In the early morning, Khalid gave himself away in front of his sisters by his unusual curiosity and repeated questions about the pretty girl who had been standing on the right of the bride. His sisters were very pleased by his interest for, although he was the eldest, he wasn't much older than his sisters, and he had never previously shown any concern for or interest in the opposite sex.

As for Hasan, the description of the girl which he gave was so airy-fairy and grandiose, all about how pretty she was, her comeliness and her charm, each sister proposed one of her favourite friends, all of whom had been at the party and whose photographs had been taken with the bride. The eldest sister said:

"There is no doubt that it is my friend Hamda for she has outstanding qualities."

The middle sister said:

"I don't think it is; Hamda didn't stay very long next to the bride. There is no doubt that he is referring to Khawla, for her beauty makes her stand out among all the others."

The youngest sister objected and said, mischieviously:

"It is neither one nor the other. Hasan is my brother and I know him well. He likes young girls and I believe that the one who has fascinated him is my classmate Shamsa, the one with the long hair."

Hasan flushed as a result of his young sister's comments. His question was unanswered by his sisters' guessing. His youngest sister said:

"Wait until the photographs come back from the studio. We sent most of the films in an hour ago."

After a short time the photographs arrived. The sisters, together with Hasan, leaped on them; this one — no; the tall one — no; the short one — no; the one with the veil — no; the one smiling — no; the dark skinned one — no; the light skinned one — no; the one wearing a green dress — no; the one with the diamond necklace — no: They went through all the photographs and the Mona Lisa did not appear in any of them. Hasan was bitterly disappointed. Then his youngest sister said that she had one more film that had not yet been developed. Hasan grabbed it and went out. An hour later he returned with all the signs of success and elation on his face. There was one picture on which the Mona Lisa appeared, showing a side view of her at the end of the film. He showed it to them but they all displayed great disappointment. Their comments came, one after the other:

"That's Buthaina, a relative of the bride."

"I don't know her."

" She is the cousin of your friend Laila."

"Very plain."

"Plump."

"Her complexion is very pallid."

"She has a wide forehead."

Hasan was delighted by her name, together with the extraordinary coincidence that had caused him to read Jamil's love ballads about Buthaina only the previous evening. But he wasn't pleased with the comments of his sisters. He left them, feeling very depressed. How stupid girls were: Buthaina, the image of the Mona Lisa, did not please them. They had commonplace, bad taste anyhow. If she had had a wide mouth like a cow, like the rest of their friends, they would have been delighted with that. And then, a narrow forehead, according to the psychologists, is a sign of an ignoble, despicable, stupid and inferior personality while a broad forehead shows nobility, strength of character and intelligence. Was a full, healthy body to be compared with a sick, skinny body ?

For the whole time while his brother and his bride were on honeymoon in Vienna and London, Hasan's mind never relaxed. The winks of Buthaina, the Mona Lisa, had robbed him of his senses and had unsettled the balance of his mind. His daily routine changed. In the ministry he paid little attention to the reports and official documents. He stopped going to the English language classes at the British Council which he had been attending for a long time. His visits to the sports club dropped off. Even when he was sitting in his favourite cafe he had a vacant look and had little to say. He devoted his time to tapes of popular music and songs which, together with those who played and sang them, he had always previously shunned. When one of his friends questioned him about the change in his taste he said he found the lyrics of colloquial love ballads attractive. Every evening, shortly before sunset, he would park his car at the entrance to the Creek and remain gazing out to sea. He had lost his heart and could think of nothing but the winks of Buthaina, the Mona Lisa, which had infatuated him and distracted him from everything and everyone else.

When his brother returned from London, Hasan talked a lot to his wife about Buthaina. She was very pleased at his curiosity especially when she came to learn that the interest and appreciation was mutual. After two days Hasan informed his mother that he wanted to marry Buthaina. Hasan's mother was not very enthusiastic about his choice but promised him that she would enquire about the girl. After looking into the matter the female camp within the family were of one mind in rejecting his choice. They set out their reasons as follows:

"There are girls among our relatives, and from the families of their friends, who were more attractive."

"She drives her own car."

"She was previously contracted to marry one of her relatives, and used to go out with him; then they broke off before the actual wedding."

"She is anaemic."

"One of her aunts is insane."

"She went away last year to Cyprus with a group of girlfriends."

Hasan scorned all their objections. What had he got to do with the girls of the family? Had there been any meeting of souls between him and any of them in the way in which his soul had embraced that of Buthaina on the night of the wedding? Had any of them bestowed upon him her winks and smiles as Buthaina had done during those few happy moments? The wife of his brother drove her own car! Half of the women in the city drove their own cars today. She did not get married because she did not feel affectionate towards the prospective bridegroom and anyway she was meant for Hasan. As for her being anaemic, that was an outright lie. Her body was full of health and vitality. Were they all blind? And what had the insanity of her aunt got to do with her? All stupid reasons and feeble excuses. Hasan became very angry. He glowered, raged and stormed, threatened and insisted on his choice. The family could find no way out but to submit to his wishes.

— 3 —

Hasan looked at Buthaina as she was feeding their son Faisal, now six weeks old. The baby did not feed continuously but would break off the suckling with little periods of cooing. This reminded him of the words of one of the Indian poets he had heard on the radio:

> *Whoever speaks about sweet music and immortal tunes*
> *has never heard the cooing of a suckling child.*

Hasan remembered the evening of the winking and smiles which, very strangely, he had never once mentioned to his wife. He said, with great tenderness, gazing dreamily into her face:
"Do you remember the wedding of my brother?"
"Yes."
"You made me so happy that night with your captivating winking."
"What winking?"
"Didn't you wink at me?"
Buthaina thought about that party and suddenly she remembered the incident. That night her car had been in the garage for repairs and she had come to the party with her neighbour Aisha. They drove with the windows open because the air-conditioning hadn't been working. When the car came out of the Shindagha tunnel it hit a sand-storm and she got some big specks of sand in her left eye. In spite of the fact that she washed it several times during the party it kept on bothering her and forced her to close her eye and wipe it so often that Aisha had said to her that she appeared as if she had only one eye.

Hasan had thought that she was winking at him. She took in the situation immediately and said, with a coy look of embarrassment: "You devil, you never forget anything."

GLOSSARY

'Aba'	Black cloak worn by Gulf ladies
'Abdulkareem Abulqadir	Famous Kuwaiti singer
'Abra	Small ferry boat
Abu	Father of
'Ali bin Rougha	Well-known singer from Abu Dhabi
Al Wasl Club	Dubai sports club
'Antar	'Antar ibn Shadaad, legendary Arab warrior
'Araq	Strong liquor, made from raisins
'Awir and Khawaneej	Settled desert areas of Dubai Emirate
Bargeel	Windtower constructed on top of house
Biriyani	Indian dish favoured by Gulf Arabs
Bisht	Cloak still worn by Gulf Arabs and others
Bismillah	Uttering the name of God
Boom	Large dhow
Burma and Karwa	Earthenware household utensils
Chanaad	King mackerel
Cordova	Quarter of Dubai, named after Arab city of Spain
Daghaiyah	Quarter of Deira, Dubai
Dhaid	A developed oasis of Sharjah Emirate

197

GLOSSARY

'Eid Al Fitr	Feast at end of fasting month of Ramadan
Ghutra	Arab headcloth
Haj	Pilgrimage to Mecca during holy month
Habouba	Sweetheart, darling
Haloosah	Local game of wits
Halwaiyo	Pilot fish
Hamriya	Area of Deira, Dubai and small port
Halba	Local herb medicine
Hareesah	Meat and whole wheat dish
Henna day	A preparation day for women before a wedding in Pakistan
Ibn Dahir	Local poet who lived in the 18th century
Imam	Leader of ritual prayers
'Iqaal	Black cord used to hold on *Ghutra*
Jameel	Arab poet of early Islamic period, the greater part of whose poetry was devoted to his beloved, Buthainah
Jash	Horse mackerel
Jinn	Invisible demons, good and bad, which affect the lives of humans
Khabaat	Mackerel
Khameer	Local bread baked with eggs added
Khor Al Ghanadhah	Area between Dubai and Abu Dhabi
Khor Khan	Creek between Dubai and Sharjah
Kohl	Substance for eye shadow
Laywa	Popular wedding dance in the Gulf
Layya	Area west of Sharjah
Mabrooka	Literally, blessed in respect of female noun